LK BILLIPS

The Catalyst

An Annabelle Sweeting Mystery

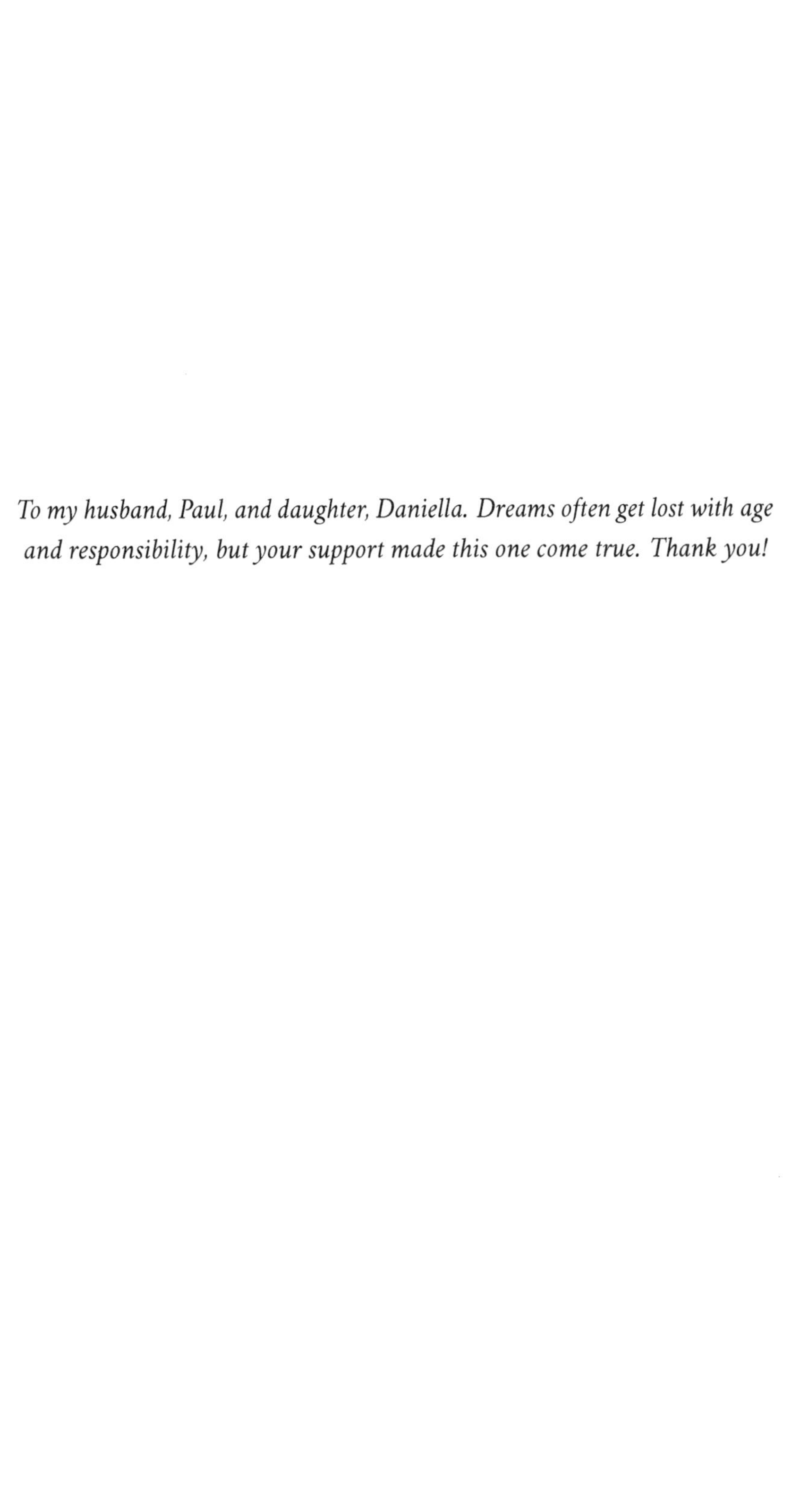

To my husband, Paul, and daughter, Daniella. Dreams often get lost with age and responsibility, but your support made this one come true. Thank you!

Contents

Acknowledgments

First and foremost, I want to thank you, the readers, for taking a chance on my story. I hope it makes you laugh, root for the heroine, and suspect everyone. Great stories are just whispers in the dark without people to tell them to.

I would like to thank Emily, Fran, Theresa, and my mom, Kathy, for their help in editing and overall support. The biggest risk to success is doubting oneself, but with friends like you, I knew I would see this through!

1

Chapter 1- New to Town

1817 – London Town- Grey skies with a chance of mayhem

I had just arrived in town and couldn't wait to embark on a most splendid season. I was to take house with my dear cousin, Jaime Nethersby, and I daresay he would make an excellent companion. My mother sent me off from our country estate in hopes that a little civilized society and the right crowd might straighten me out from my mechanically inclined mind and bookish desires. 'Pish posh and hogwash,' I would say, but never to her face.

Her life-long dream of living away from society and enjoying the fresh air had long since been realized. I, however, had wanted to see the industry and the cogs and gears of the great town of London since I could first have a rational thought. My cousin, Jaime, I understand, is quite peculiar as well. He has a tendency to dress quite brightly, and I daresay he loves feathers to the extent of exhaustion. There was an indication that we would be rivals in the romance arena, but I think that would be most intriguing.

Stepping off from the Steam Engine No. 7, I walked across the platform searching for my luggage. I traveled light. I had hoped to come across some splendid fabrics upon my journey to make a truly fetching ensemble. Yes, I make my own clothes. I know that is not "ton" etiquette, but I love putting my own touches on things. Perhaps the addition of mechanized moving parts is a bit much, but I do so love to make brooches and hairpins that whirl. I had one such piece firmly attached to the traveling hat I was wearing. It was a flattened brass sparrow shown as if in-flight with moving metal wings, and I used a wind-up mechanism from an old timepiece. I loved the ticking noise it made as I moved through the crowd.

I stepped lightly and made my way to the cargo cart. A scurry behind me caught my attention as three guttersnipes weaved in and out. One bumped me on his way, and I quickly grasped the back of his collar and brought him to a halt.

"Return it at once," I demanded of the little thief. "You are quite skilled, but I have worked hard for the little I have, and you will not benefit from my toil."

The child stared at me in utter awe. I doubt he had ever been caught before. He unfolded his hand, and there was my small purse. It had been tucked neatly in the side of my skirt, and I was surprised he had extricated it. I took the pouch and felt the weight of it. I bent down to peer into his eyes.

"Give me the rest, you are not fooling me." His eyes widened in shock. He dropped the two coins he had liberated from my purse into my outstretched hand. "What do you have to say for yourself?"

"Sawry misses, I thought you were a Glimmer. Didn't expect you'd be a Brass wit' a fancy hawt like that," he responded.

"A Glimmer? What is that, little one?"

"You know, a fancy to do with the nawt a care in the world since they so rich. Always cover'd in such shiny things." He gestured as if his hands were covered in rings. "But you are like us, a Brass, a working stiff."

"I daresay thieving is not working at all young sir, and you should find yourself some appropriate employment before you end up in Scotland Yard, or worse, the gallows."

He shifted from his left to right foot and made an audible gulp as he contemplated what fate I would deal him. I smirked and tapped my chin with the hand still holding the purse.

"I think I have just the thing for you. Come now and grab my bags. You will be my assistant while I am in town and tell me all such things that I do not know. In return, you will not go to the gallows, and I will pay you a fair wage. What do you say?"

His eyes looked at me bewildered and weary as if I was toying with him and would call for the constable any moment. His eyes darted back and forth, looking for his fellow snipes, and having found them being pinched by the aforementioned, he turned to me and nodded most fervently.

A tap on my left shoulder had me turning to face a most handsome constable. He stood about five inches taller than me and had dark brown hair and eyes. His face, although clean-shaven, looked to have a perpetual five o'clock shadow. I had a curious urge to feel the texture of it. I blinked rapidly with the direction my thoughts had taken. Shaking myself loose from the momentary lapse in composure, I released my hold on the boy and curtsied to the constable.

"Hello sir, what is it I can assist you with?" I asked calmly.

The boy could've run but instead sidled up beside me as if to show a solid front. I peeked down at him and gave him a firm nod. He returned the gesture, and I knew my bargain had been accepted.

"Not sir, miss… what I mean to say is I'm Constable Weston, and I am here to apprehend this urchin for pick-pocketing," he said. "I can see you have done the hard work for me by capturing his collar."

"Sir— I mean Constable Weston, I am Miss Annabelle Sweeting and this is my traveling boy. I am afraid you are mistaken about his misdeeds. He did say quite a coarse word that resulted in the collar grab, but he assured me he would act more civilized once we reached my cousin's. Boy, introduce yourself to the constable."

The boy's eyes looked large as saucers as his lips trembled with fear. He took a deep breath in and steadied himself quite amiably before looking at the constable.

"I am Nathan Starling. Constable, I am employed now by Miss Sweeting and will be off to get her bags if there is nawt else, sir?" He bowed most gallantly, took my luggage ticket, and hurried off to the waiting bag attendant.

Turning my attention back to Constable Weston, I looked him up and down from head to toe. Noticing the scuff on his hat on the left side, the loose button on his wrist, and the extremely shiny yet worn boots, I could tell this man was a bachelor. Why this mattered to me, I do not know, but I felt relieved by it. He cleared his throat audibly and smirked when my eyes met his dark brown stare. I felt my cheeks heat from being caught observing and quickly covered my embarrassment with a smile.

"Thanks again, Constable Weston, I am sure you have more pressing issues to tend to now that you are aware there is nothing amiss here. Thank you kindly for the inquiry", I said dismissively.

"Of course, Miss Sweeting, and should you need my services while you're in town, please take my card," he said, stopping me from turning away with his extended hand. I reached for his card, our fingers brushed, and we both dropped the card. Eyes connecting instantly, we both bent down to retrieve the fallen card, trying to deny the electric pulse that had just occurred. Eyes never wavering, we came up simultaneously holding the card on each end.

"Ahem, miss, I've got yawrs luggage if you're all ready?" Little Nate, bless his heart, breaking the awkward trance I'd found myself in.

"I do apologize, Constable Weston, I don't know what happened there, perhaps the journey has caught up to me. Thank you for your card and we shall be off now." I hastily gathered my parasol and began to walk towards the exit. Nathan did his best to keep up with my luggage. I dared not look back, fearful of what I would see. I had no idea why a young, helpful constable might be frightening to me in the least.

2

Chapter 2- The Bustling City

Just a weary traveler or completely out of my head? Verdict still out.

We finally reached the street outside the train station. I took a big breath of air and tried to relieve myself of this unknown emotion that had enveloped me. Instead, I found myself choking on the dirty steam of a passing vehicle.

"Miss, are ye alright? You look like you've swallowed a cotton ball." Nathan patted me on the back as hard as his tiny hands could muster.

"Yes, yes, just not used to this city air quite yet. Thank you, Nathan, for your assistance. Let us hail a motor and head straight to Bread Street. My cousin shall be anticipating my arrival there shortly."

"Bread Street, miss? I thought you wasn't a Glimmer? Sounds a bit fancy ta-doo." He raised his eyebrow questioningly to me.

"My cousin does seem to run in higher circles, but I had not thought much on it. Growing up in the country, society was neither here nor there. We shall have to acquaint ourselves together in that realm of the ton, I suppose, Nathan. I care not really what they think of me, but it would be dreadful to hurt my cousin's standing by mistake."

Nathan brought his two fingers to his mouth and let out a shrill whistle. Although painful on the ears, the sound was quite effective in getting noticed. A rather banged up yet shiny motor pulled up next to the curb and waited. Inside was the most exotic looking man I had ever seen. His skin was shiny and tanned to the hue of almonds. His hair, dark as pitch and shoulder-length, was tied up in a leather strap. The most striking was his eyes, though. They were peridot, cat-like in shape, and practically glowing with the reflection of the sun. Awestruck, I openly gaped and wondered what paint I could use to replicate that beautiful green.

"Where to, miss?" he said as he leaned out his window. His buttery words came to rest with a sly smirk. Collecting myself, I shook my head gently.

"I apologize, I was.. have never seen quite a hue." I stumbled, and Nathan caught my elbow and righted me. The motor driver openly smiled now.

"I know my skin can be quite shocking, but no cause for alarm I assure you."

"Oh no, not shocking, I assure you," I stammered. "I was actually referring to your most unique and beautiful eyes." I caught myself leaning in to get a better look and couldn't help but blush. "I apologize once again, ah yes, we need to go to Bread Street, please. Nathan, please put my bags in the back." I tried to collect myself, looking anywhere but directly at his face. Nathan loaded my traveling bags in the boot, and the driver hopped out of his door and opened the back for me.

"Here you are, miss. My name is Miro, and may I say your eyes are quite fetching as well." The teasing in his voice was evident, and I couldn't help but laugh at myself. I really did not seem to know how to act today.

"A pleasure Miro, I seem to be a little out of character from my travels, but I am sure you will forget the whole scene once we are parted. I am Miss Annabelle Sweeting, and this here is Nathan Starling." Nathan climbed in the back as the driver took his spot in front.

"Sweeting and Starling, now that seems like a formidable team, indeed. And, miss, no one who has met you would forget you any time soon. I can assure you of that," he said with a wink.

I felt the heat creep up my neck as we pulled away from the curb. I would surely disgrace my cousin if I kept this act up. Chiding myself, I stared blankly out the window until the scenery started to penetrate my reverie. The city was filled with the most wondrous things. Little propelled gizmos fluttered next to a street vendor, and motorized spiral staircases could be seen through transparent walls winding their way up to the higher-level boutiques. The smell of steam and glazed hazelnuts assaulted my senses in the most enticing way. I sighed and closed my eyes, enjoying the sensation. Opening my eyes, I found that a pair of green ones were staring back at me from the side mirror. They were intense and alarming, and I smiled sheepishly. I sat back in my seat to escape their gaze.

We pulled up to my cousin's place, and Nathan hopped out to get the luggage. I reached for my own door and found Miro opening it concurrently. He looked down at me with the same intensity, and I felt a shiver of something I could not place. He offered his hand, and I took it hesitantly.

"No, Miss Annabelle Sweeting. Not any time soon, indeed," he said.

He lifted my hand to his lips and gave it a parting kiss. Nathan handed him his fee, and the next thing I knew, the motor was racing down the road. It wasn't until he turned the corner that I understood his words. A smile spread across my face. A most exceedingly intriguing start to this journey.

3

Chapter 3- My Cousin's Dwelling

Is it me, or can one like feathers a little too much? Asking for a friend.

We walked up the stairs to my cousin's house, and I took in the bright bouquets of flowers in the window boxes. Such cheery blooms gleamed on a rather grey street. I smiled as Nathan hit the button beside the door. Chimes began to sound, and a whizzing of gears and pulleys began to move. Steam plumed out from the top as the doors swung inward to reveal a butler in the most jaw-dropping ensemble I had ever seen. Bright canary yellow with a peach waist sash stood out first. But nothing could prepare my eyes for the feathered delight upon his head. He grimaced as he followed the direction of my eyes to the hat of yellow plumage he was sporting.

"May I help you, miss?"

"Oh yes, I am Miss Annabelle Sweeting, and I have come to stay with Jaime, oh, I mean my cousin, well, Mr. Nethersby," I said, trying to remove my focus from the dazzling accessory.

"Cousin, cousin, is that you, at last?" I could hear Jaime shouting from within. He came rushing to the door and scooped me up, spinning me in a circle. I laughed as he kissed both my cheeks and smiled down at

9

me. His outfit was no less impressive than his butler's. He wore olive green with gold paisley detailing and a cravat with a peacock feather pinned to it. I turned towards Nathan to find his mouth open, and his gaze swiveled from Jaime to the butler and back again. I gently lifted his chin and set to the introductions.

"Dear cousin, it is great to see you again. This lad here is Nathan Starling, and he is now in my employ."

"Oh dear, Belle, you always loved taking in strays. Tsk, Tsk these rags will not do for my cousin's traveling boy. We shall have to go shopping straight away," he said. A look of horror flashed upon Nathan's face.

"Actually, cousin, I will take this task on myself, as I must procure some fabrics for my own ensembles, and I am already indebted to your kindness for hosting me here. Where are the best silk shops, do you suppose?" My question deliberately diverted Jaime's attention from Nathan, and the boy gave me a grateful smile. We walked through the door, and my cousin rattled off several places he thought would be suitable for my clothing selections. After rapturing over my hat, Jaime told me of a local gear shop that would serve my needs as well.

We walked and chatted amiably about our plans for the season. I then took in the room where we stood. I gasped at the pure decadence of it. Fabrics were rich red with silver threading, and dark wood furniture sprinkled the room. Each room we passed had a different theme of patterns and colors. It was truly a sight to feast upon.

"If you like this, you'll love what I did to your room!" He took me by the hand, and we moved quickly up the stairs. "I know this is quite ill decorum cousin, but we have always been odd, and I think it suits us. Perhaps, in public, we will put on our droll faces, but I hope you permit my whimsy in our shared quarters?" He looked at me with hopeful and nervous eyes.

"Of course, cousin, why do you think I accepted this invitation? Stuffy

Aunt Prudence has been trying to get me out here for years, but I would not do well, I think, under her tutelage," I replied. We looked at each other for a second and started laughing heartily.

"Yes, yes, Prud is quite that, isn't she? Bless her heart!" He then opened the door to my room and waited with bated breath for my reaction. A beautiful posted bed stood gleaming in the center of the space. A glossy, warm wood finish with gorgeous light rose hues gave it a meadowy look. Furniture of the same warm wood placed around the room gave it a cozy feel, and rose brass accents gleamed in the light of the fireplace. Mechanical brass fixtures adjoined the window to pulleys, opening to a private balcony overlooking the small back garden. I looked back into my cousin's eyes and leaped at him with a hug.

"It's truly a work of art! You are too good to me."

"Belle, you've always been kind to me, even when our family has been quite unfeeling. I've had good fortune since father died, and I could not dream of sharing it with anyone more deserving than you. We shall have great adventures, I believe. And come the end of the season, if you haven't grown tired of my company, you are welcome to stay on as long as your heart desires. Just don't make me too jealous with all those dashing beaus that are sure to be calling soon," he said.

"I know it's been hard for you, Jaime. Especially, with the way the ton is predisposed to gossip. I can only offer my promise to never look at you differently than I always have. As I really don't see the problem with it at all. Just that we may be competitive from time to time." I said with a wink. "I will try to not do anything embarrassing either to bring attention from the gossip mongers. I would not dream of disparaging your name with how hard you've worked to get here. Working with the top dressmaker in town is no small feat, indeed!"

"My dear, your concern for me is heartwarming. I don't worry about what they say too much. What can be worse than what my own family has said? I daresay you could not embarrass me even if you fell on your head in the middle of Almack's. You are the only family I really count now," he said. He then kissed my forehead and walked down towards his own living quarters. "Afternoon tea once you are settled, okay?"

I nodded and headed back inside the beauty that was my room. Nathan struggled up the stairs with my bags, brought them in, and set them in the corner. He looked around and let out a low whistle. "Well, Miss Sweeting, I'd say you waz a Glimmer now for sure."

"I daresay, you might just be right, Nate. Now, go down to the kitchen and get yourself something to eat. You must be famished from hauling my luggage. Please send up a maid to fill my tub. I must get this travel grime off me at once. You could also do with a good washing. Tomorrow we will set out on the town and collect what we need to make our season's styles, I think," I mused.

"You mean to make clothes for me, ma'am? I donna know what to say. Don't Glimmers get clothes made for 'em? Perhaps, you should do the same, now you are moved up in the world. You don't need worry about me," he spoke shyly.

"Nonsense! They have nothing that I want. I make what pleases me, and if that is Brass then I guess that is what I shall remain to be. You and I are a team now. A formidable one, apparently. So we shall dress the part. Unless you like your rags and do not like my style?" I questioned.

"Oh no, miss, that is, your style is gleaming. I have naught seen the like of such tinkering before." He pulled his hat off and placed it on his chest. "I'd be honored, undeservin', but honored for such fancy ta-doo."

"It's settled then," I said.

He smiled wide at me. He scampered out of the room and headed to do what he was asked. Flopping down upon the bed, I felt lighthearted and relieved to find myself here at last. I closed my eyes, and two different sets of eyes clouded my thoughts. One was dark quizzical brown, the other intensely green.

4

Chapter 4- Ribbons, Ribbons Everywhere

Tell me the truth, does this poufy dress make me look fat? Yes, yes, it does.

The morning started out with the most delicious scones I had ever tasted. Jaime left early to meet his employer and promised to dine with me in the afternoon. Nathan and I set off on foot towards the shops Jaime said would be most promising.

The weather was brisk and foggy, but still visible. The market was just setting up their displays as we passed by. Fresh vegetable stands edged up to wonderful trinket vendors. One such vendor stood out with a dashing studded leather eye patch and the most fetching leather belts and buckles strapped across his chest. His wares consisted of intricate timepieces, fluttering mechanical butterflies, and some rather ornate spring action daggers. I stopped and inquired on where he purchased his leather pieces. He indicated that the leather shop he frequented was located just next to the gear shop we intended to visit. As we were headed off, he grasped my hand.

"Before you go, miss, please take this. I donna why, but you will need it," he warned.

He placed a metal bracer decorated with red jeweled pegs in my hand.

13

He then adhered it upon my wrist and pressed down on one of the pegs. A secret compartment opened, and a small thin dagger sprung to attention.

"Oh no, sir, I couldn't possibly…" I stammered.

"Trust me, miss. There's a feeling about you. I cannot in good conscience let you go without." He looked between Nathan and me with unease.

"Well, I must pay you for it then."

I pushed the dagger back into its hidey-hole and began digging through my purse. He halted my hand. He pointed to my brooch of moving flower petal gears. It took me quite a bit of rummaging to find the pieces to make it, but I found myself unpinning the pin and handing it to him without protest. Something strange and eerie was happening, and I couldn't quite shake the feeling that he was right. Nathan grabbed my elbow and pulled me back as I continued to stare at this man's one good eye.

"Miss, are you alright? That's One-eyed Whitmore, and he's said to be some sort of witch. I've ne'er seen him down here before. He stays mostly in the Brass Borough. He's a dangerous sort, folks say, telling tales of curses and missing folks." Nathan shuddered as he spoke. "I'm not sure you should have taken anything from the likes of him, miss."

"I can't explain it, Nate, but I feel like it was all predetermined. I'm not quite sure what it all means, but I hope this doesn't bode ill for the near future."

We continued to walk towards the first fabric shop on our list. Bethany's Boutique had a wooden sign painted with bold purple and silver highlights. The bell chimed as we entered, and I was surprised to see several other customers out this early. A woman and her two daughters were, what I can only describe as, accosting a poor sales girl with bolts of fabric and ribbon. They halted their efforts as our presence was noticed.

"I thought my daughters were the only appointment today. We will not be rushed in our fitting, and you can assure Miss Bethany of that!"

The woman turned and huffed, walking past us toward the back fitting area. The salesgirl trailed her with the heavy burden and gave me an apologetic smile.

She returned moments later and, with a curtsy, explained that there were to be no other fittings available today.

"That is fine. Miss Bethany, is it?"

"Ah, not the miss, I'm Eleanor, her apprentice," she blushed. "Miss Bethany is seeing to Mrs. Cosswald and her daughters now. They can be quite…particular about their season fashions."

"I understand, Eleanor, and I will not detain you from fitting. I only wish to peruse your fabrics. When I have chosen the ones I like, can I summon you to purchase them?"

"Aye, but you don't need a fitting, yourself? I'm sure if you came back we could make you an excellent set of dresses," she said.

"Actually, I tend to my own attire, so that service shall not be required." I smiled as she lifted a brow.

"Fine by me, miss?" she questioned.

"I am Annabelle Sweeting, and I am staying with my cousin, Mr. Nethersby, on Bread Street. I will need the lengths purchased delivered there. Will that be a problem?"

"Mr. Nethersby! Oh, I will let Miss Bethany know you are here, and no, no that should not be a problem at all." She rushed out of the room, and I was left pondering why my cousin's name should invoke such energy. Perhaps, he has more status than he conveyed due to his employer.

I set to the task of filtering through the lovely shades of silk and linen and wool, oh my! Nathan trailed in my wake in utter awe at the magnitude of colors the fabrics came in.

"What's your favorite color, Nathan? You look like a dove grey to me," I said.

"I've never thought about it much miss, I wear what I can find," he replied.

"Well then, we shall have to guess for a while and see what sticks. Here, I will add the ones I like for you, and you go stack them up on the counter," I directed.

As we made our way through the color wheel, I came out with several stunning shades of lavender, reds, blues, browns, and greys. I've found the darker hues worked well with my fair skin, dark chestnut hair, and matching eyes. Lavender was a guilty pleasure, and the greys, blues, and browns would suit Nathan too.

We were scanning through some ribbon accent pieces when a lovely woman emerged from the back. She wore a rose-colored dress with lace accents and floral brass buttons. Her warm smile greeted us as she walked over.

"Miss Sweeting, I apologize for not coming out sooner, but my current client is very...particular, and begs all of my attention on such days," she started.

"Ah, Miss Bethany, your store is quite wonderful. I thought I might have to go to several fabric places, but it seems my cousin was right to tell me to stop here first. It is no bother at all, I do not need much attention and was just about done with our selections. You will find all the fabrics on the counter and paper pinned to each one with the amount needed. I presume that will suffice?" I asked.

Miss Bethany walked over to the counter and looked through my selections.

"Oh my, well if you ever need a job, I daresay, look no further. Such detailed notes. Yes, this is perfect. I will have them delivered this week and put to your cousin's account as directed," she said.

"My cousin's account? Oh, no! I will pay the bill when it is ready."

"I'm sorry, Miss Sweeting, but your cousin specifically told me not to let you pay a pence. I dare not get on his bad side. You wouldn't wish that, would you?" she said with a mock pout.

I did not want to get her in trouble, so I would have to find some way to pay Jaime back. I shook my head no at her questioning expression.

"Thank you for your help, Miss Bethany, and good luck…"

I was cut off by the entrance of the two daughters from the back in poufy, massively ill-functioning dresses in matching shades of pea green. I heard Nathan audibly gasp at the vision before us and then snicker.

"Miss Cara, Miss Whitney, how do you like the dresses your mother has commissioned for you?" Miss Bethany asked, starting towards them.

"Miss Bethany, they are spectacular! Can you add a bow to mine and a flower to Whitney's so they are just a tad different?" Miss Cara requested.

Miss Whitney started to strut through the store or, at least, waddle with panache. She gave me a haughty look as she passed and said, "We will be all the rage this season, no one will touch the elegance of our attire for sure, sister. These will surely get Mr. Nethersby's attention. Ooh, can I get a matching feather hat?"

Nathan and I looked at each other in disbelief. With a shake of my head, I indicated to Miss Bethany that revealing my relation to Jaime was unnecessary. The two girls continued to twirl and flounce about the front room as we took our leave. We headed out the door swiftly and made our way down the lane. I chuckled to myself, thinking that the dagger One-eyed Whitmore gave me was to fend off the acquaintance of the Cosswald sisters.

5

Chapter 5- A Most Absurd Meeting

A wolf in sheep's clothing? Surely, someone so good-looking couldn't be so dastardly.

The leather shop proved very rewarding, as did the gear shop. Upon picking out items for the gear shop, I made sure to inform the owner that I would be handling billing. That, no matter what my cousin had said, I would pay, or I would not purchase at all. He begrudgingly said he would honor my request. In addition, the shop owner also told me that the local metalsmith discards pieces every week he doesn't think are suitable for his work. If I headed down two blocks and followed the steamy heat, I could catch today's excess. *What luck!* I thought.

We weaved our way through the mounting crowd and towards the back alley of the metal warehouse. Nathan was quite inept at the task. There seemed to be all kinds of splendid bits to play with. Once Nathan ran out of space in his pockets, I unfixed my travel bonnet and started to load that up as well. A tinkerer's daydream.

The head metalsmith, Charles Kaplan, seemed amused by my enthusiasm. He offered a rucksack for my use, and in exchange, I promised to make him a new set of goggles that would auto-wipe the steam buildup while he worked. A valuable friendship, I knew, had just been forged. To keep my word, I headed off to a glass shop and picked out several shaded lenses in a few different hues. Walking outside, I peered through the red lens towards the sun to gauge its shading capacity. I heard scuffling on my left and turned just in time to see two men barreling down the walk in our direction. These men were not the type to be behaving this way, as they were dressed to impress with perfectly tailored suits. I jumped back as they tumbled down and took the place I had just stood. Looking up panting, a flicker of recognition flashed in a pair of intense green eyes.

"Miss Sweeting!" Miro exclaimed. He quickly picked himself up and brushed the dirt off the front of his jacket. He turned to his counterpart and offered him a hand up.

"I apologize for that little display of brotherly disaffection. Let me introduce you to my eldest brother Lord Oliver Nassar, Earl of Thetford."

Lord Thetford stepped forward and took my hand, bowing over it. "Miss Annabelle Sweeting, it is a pleasure to meet you and forgive us. My brother and I had a small disagreement, but being a passionate pair, we clearly let it get out of hand." He looked towards Miro with a smirk while still holding my hand.

I gently withdrew my hand and said, "Lord Thetford, it is likewise a pleasure to meet you. Miro did not mention a brother, but then again, we did not talk long in our short meeting yesterday. Strange that the brother of an earl should be bussing people from the train in his motor. Then again, far stranger things have happened to me today. Oh, I apologize, I am rambling, aren't I? " He had the same exotic look as his brother. A little shorter but with the same almond skin. His eyes, still catlike, were an amber hue.

"You are correct in your assessment of my little brother. I am quite scandalized to hear of his common cabbie expeditions. Brother, what is the meaning of this?" He turned to Miro with an accusatory stare. Miro simply shrugged and gave me a wink.

"How else am I to meet pretty girls, Oliver? You with the title, I am usually overlooked," he pouted.

After not receiving the sympathetic response he was hoping for, he continued. "Okay, I was testing out the motor George and I are building for the race in a couple weeks. I know you disapprove of my hobby brother, but the Motor Gala is the talk of the ton, and it is very prestigious to be accepted into the race," he exclaimed.

His brother just glared, clearly curbing the retort he had in mind. "Hobbies aside, how does that explain your pickup of dear Miss Sweeting?" he asked.

"Ah, well that was all luck and happenstance. I was driving back from the track and heard the shrillest whistle that I hit the brakes reflectively and saw the most interesting lady standing on the curb." My face flushed as he continued. "I couldn't very well pass up the opportunity of making a new acquaintance, now could I? And since the cat's out of the bag, I can return your payment, Miss Sweeting, as I am not officially a cabbie," he said.

"You took her money? What kind of crazed lunatic do I have for a brother? I do apologize, Miss Sweeting, I assure you my brother will not be causing such mayhem going forward." He grimaced at Miro.

"Miss Sweeting, you're not mad at me, are you?" Miro asked.

"No, but I must take greater care when entering a motor from now on, I daresay. The tag you had in your vehicle looked quite genuine. I would hate to get into a dire predicament with another impostor!"

Looking abashed, Miro replied, "Yes, yes, I am sorry, it was an official tag. It belongs to my co-mechanic, George. He usually drives the transport, but I was taking liberties that day and may have gotten carried away. Do forgive me!"

"Only if you promise utter honesty from this day forth? I truly cannot tolerate being deceived!"

"Take it from me, sir," Nathan chimed in, "she does not tolerate it one bit!" I smiled over to my little champion.

"Miss Sweeting, there will be a party two nights hence at our estate that I hope you will attend, I am sure you should have received the invitation for you and your cousin by now. I wish to make amends for my behavior," Miro said shyly.

"Honourable Nassar, I will discuss this with my cousin this afternoon and reply accordingly." I smiled at the formality of his name. "Nathan and I must take our leave now, as I am off to meet my cousin for tea. I bid you both farewell." They both bowed, and I turned on my heels with Nathan trailing behind.

A feeling overwhelmed me; if I didn't leave then, I would seriously consider strangling Miro's deceptive neck. Or accepting the party invite right then and there. Both decisions, I needed to think a little more on. I hate being made a fool, especially by such a handsome devil. I shook my head to dismiss the last part of that statement. Well, except for the devil part. That is for sure.

6

Chapter 6- Talk of the Town

There is nothing quite like the perfect cup of tea, nothing!

After that strange display in the street, I couldn't wait to meet my cousin for lunch and discuss all that had occurred. Nathan and I weaved our way through the streets and entered the bistro my cousin had designated. It was named Claymore's, after the owner, and boasted having the best meat pies in the district. I cannot convey how much I adore meat pies.

We made our way to his table and sat down with our packages. Jaime laughed at our bedraggled appearance and had his servant fetched to relay our goods to Bread Street. We ordered the famed meat pies and dived into our morning's adventures while we waited.

"And, they were just wrestling on the ground in front of you? And, this was before or after you met the horrid Lady Cosswalds? Oh dear, perhaps I should have accompanied you on your first day out?"

Jaime's clouded expression had me in a fit of giggles.

"What is so funny, cousin?"

"Oh Jaime, your concern for me is unfounded. If I can handle old Mr. Winterstile, my father's very peculiar cattle master, no oddity can scathe me. I can deal perfectly well on my own. I do, however, concede on the deception of Mr. Nassar. You know how I loathe falsehoods. I usually get to the bottom of them, but I did not see that one coming." I looked at him with pinched brows.

"Perhaps, you were too distracted by the visual pleasures before you?" His teasing smirk provoked me.

Before I could reply, our food arrived. I was saved from giving a falsehood of my own. We ate in deliberate silence, both peeking at each other, waiting for whatever mischief the other had planned. A fresh pot of tea was laid on our table when I finally broke the silence.

"Well, I suppose we could go to this party we've been invited to. I understand it will be full of need-to-know people and some possible new clientele for you. I should have something suitable to wear by then if you don't mind me setting up in your study or a spare bedroom. I've never been to such a party, so I would like the experience of it. Unless, you think it will not be fun?" I looked at him in question.

"You will have to work on your coyness, dear cousin. You are not sly at all. Of course, we will go. I can't wait to see this Lord Thetford and Honourable Nassar myself, and with the apparent splash you've made on society so far, I know the invites will be raining in afterward. Now, let us savor this tea and tell me more about this Charles fellow with the large, um, hammer. I think I've seen him about the smith warehouse. Does he have blond hair by chance, and a constant five o'clock shadow?" Jaime wiggled his eyebrows suggestively at me.

I laughed out loud and told him more about the head metalsmith. When I finished the new goggles, I promised Jaime he could accompany me in making their delivery. My cousin was quite pleased, indeed. I realized I had forgotten to tell him all about the strange man with the eye patch and the new bracer dagger I now adorn.

"Jaime, what do you think of this piece?" He eyed the bracelet and removed it from my wrist.

"It looks a little extravagant for your taste, Belle, where did you get it?"

"I got it from a dashing gentleman in an eye patch named… What was his name, Nathan?" I turned to look at the boy.

"One-eyed Whitmore. I told her nawt to talk to him, but she's a power, sir," he stammered.

Jaime looked at me to Nate and back again. "What did he say to you, Belle? They claim he has premonition powers and to heed his words. Others say he's just a loon. I like to think there is still magic in this world, though," he said.

I clicked the peg on the bracelet to release the dagger's hidden compartment and watched as Jaime's mouth fell open.

"He told me that I would need this and that I couldn't leave without taking it. I traded him my gear flower brooch for it. I just couldn't walk away. It was like an eerie trance or something." I shivered with the memory of it.

"Oh my, well put it back on. I hope his words are empty. It is a shame about that brooch though, it was one of your beauties, for sure. Perhaps, he will trade something else for it? I will try to find him and see if he will bargain." We finished our tea and left Claymore's and its enticing smells behind.

The two nights that followed were spent in a flurry trying to get outfits suitable for Nathan and me to wear to the party. Nathan Starling polished up quite well, indeed. I fashioned him with light tan pants, brass fasteners, and a dark leather belt. Several more belts were added, with buckles along the left leg where he could access hidden pockets. I gave him a dark leather vest with two buttons made of scrap lead and a scarab pin made of gears with legs that wiggled. He really liked that part. I also gave Nate a porcupine hat and fixed a copper starling to the side that blinked its sapphire eyes every hour. His eyes appeared to mist up when I handed it to him, but he claimed he was having a bout of allergies.

I fixed myself up a delicious number of lavender and warm suede accents. As this was a party, I opted for a skirt of the silky purple material, but only a half skirt in the front and buckskin-colored pants below. They had copper buttons along the seams of the pant legs and matching buttons in two rows down the front of the bodice. I made a crown of mechanical butterflies with functional wings for my hair. The butterflies had purple and red glass accents and matched my dress and dagger bracer.

7

Chapter 7- Dinner Party

What can I say? I love a good....refreshment!

We arrived at the Thetford Estate to find a line of motors patiently waiting their turn to unload. The steam encompassed the roadway like a fog setting in on a gothic novel. I observed each guest exit their vehicles, make their way up the stairs, and through the open door filled with light. Each person was cataloged; the detail of their dress, the manner of their walking, and the height they held their chin. Some people I couldn't wait to meet. Others, I felt I would need a closer review from a distance.

They say you should not judge a book by its cover, but I daresay you can see a lot from the packaging, indeed. You can detect what they wish to portray, minute indications in their mannerism of how they really are, and, of course, how well they pull off the act.

Our turn finally arrived, and Jaime leaped out, reaching back for my hand. As I grasped it and took several steps, I heard a gasp from my left and turned to find two sets of haughty eyes staring back at me from pea-green clad ladies. My cousin followed my attention and sneaked me a wink before pulling me forward to formally meet the Cosswald

Sisters.

"Lady Whitney and Lady Cara, you are both looking exceedingly well tonight. That green is quite eye-catching, and of course, I never say no to feathers," Jaime cooed.

This flattery brought sighs from both their lips, and they smiled at him adoringly. "Ah, yes. I've heard you ran into my cousin here at Bethany's the other morning. Let me formally introduce you. This is Miss Annabelle Sweeting."

I curtsied customarily, trying to conceal my amused expression. "Nice to meet you, Miss Cosswalds. I must agree with my cousin, Miss Bethany did an extraordinary job on your ensembles. I can't wait to see what other delightful creations you've all come up with," I said earnestly.

Miss Cara stepped forward, taking me by surprise by grabbing my hand and saying, "Oh, Miss Sweeting, it is a pleasure to meet you. Had we known the other day that you were a cousin to dear Mr. Nethersby, we would have introduced ourselves properly. You must come to take tea with us and tell us all about your trip so far. How long are you planning to visit?"

Miss Whitney perked up at this and leaned in to catch my reply. Her face lit up with the hope of my quick departure.

" I will stay for the entire season Miss Cara, and my cousin has allowed me to stay on after the season if I do not have a place of my own by then," I replied.

"Oh cousin, you will not leave my comfortable arrangements to get a small apartment in Brass Boroughs! No, indeed. You will stay with me until we both die or some dastardly beau steals you away and convinces you to marry him," Jaime exclaimed. The expression on Miss Whitney's face changed several times between surprise, confusion, and ultimately the impression that she had tasted a rather potent lemon.

"Oh, but Mr. Nethersby, you would want her to have her own abode when you take the wedding plunge, I am sure?" Cara questioned.

"I'm sure that if that day comes, any partner of mine would be happy to have Miss Sweeting stay on," he said assertively.

"I must say, that is quite an intriguing crown upon your head, Miss Sweeting. Where did you buy it?" Miss Whitney finally chimed in after being assured I had no romantic claim on Jaime. "And your dress is like nothing we have seen in the shops," she added.

"Thank you, Miss Cosswald. I made them myself," I replied.

"Yeah, and she made mine too, isn't she great, mum?" Nathan chimed in, pushing himself to my side to show off his new duds.

"That is quite industrious of you, Miss Sweeting," she replied haughtily. "Perhaps, we could commission a few pieces?"

"I thank you, Miss Cosswald," I replied stiffly. "I plan to open a shop here, eventually. For now, though, I only do it for my own enjoyment and for friends and family." Point made, I curtsied and took my cousin's arm to be led into the lion's den.

A lion, indeed. Cunning and sly from the start. Even now, I thought I could feel those green eyes haunting my steps. Looking up, I saw that my feeling had been correct. I wondered how long Mr. Nassar had been observing me.

We reached the landing without any other interruption and greeted the hosting brothers. I made introductions to my cousin, and we entered the ballroom to the left. Clearly, whatever profession these two capitalized in was treating them very well. The high ceilings opened in two sections by a motorized system leaving the night sky in view. Tall iron lions flanked the sides of the room with kerosene lanterns perched from their open maws.

The refreshment table was serviced by a flurry of flying bots in the shape of different animals of legend pouring the brightest colored drinks I had ever seen. A most ravishing mermaid served a beautiful sapphire lemonade to a man facing away from me. I watched as she finished pouring the drink and fluttered her tail as she flew away.

The man seemed familiar, but I could not tell from where. He has dressed in dove gray breeches with several leather straps across his waist and lavender suspenders. As if answering my request for him to turn to finish my assessment, he did.

A leather bracer timepiece was strapped to his left forearm, and a matching leather shoulder armor adorned his right arm. A lavender handkerchief was tied around his neck. His hair, not quite shaggy, jutted out in the most flattering manner. Finally, I rested my eyes upon his face and was shocked to see who stared back at me.

"Ding dong cousin, who is that fetching piece of manhood eyeing you up from the refreshment table? Seems someone is keeping secrets already," Jaime whispered.

"Oh, I forgot to tell you of how I met Nathan at the train station, and how that handsome gentleman is a constable who tried to apprehend Nate for pickpocketing. Although he deserved it, I saved dear Nate from the gallows and thus earned his servitude. I daresay I won out on the bargain. He has refused payment," I said.

"Belle, I swear you are too generous by half! Well, I do agree Nathan Starling has made an excellent companion for you and seems to know a great deal about the city. Right now, I see him scanning from the corner, making sure you are alright. What a dear boy," he complied.

Grabbing my cousin's arm, I headed towards Constable Weston in the hopes of discovering why such an event would require the law here. His dark eyes kept pace with my advance. We reached the refreshment table, and a mechanical manticore circled my head sniffing my butterfly headpiece. He flew off after being beckoned by another guest. Constable Weston smiled at our approach.

"Constable Weston, I am surprised to see you here, is there crime afoot?" I said. "This is my cousin, Mr. Jaime Nethersby, the executive assistant to the famous designer, Lady Cornelia Whipley. Cousin, this is Constable Weston, whom I met when I first arrived at the train station."

"Good to see you again, Miss Sweeting. Outside the uniform, I am Mr. Luke Weston, nephew to Lady Whipley, and it is a great pleasure to meet you, Mr. Nethersby, as I've recently heard a lot about you," he said with a chuckle. "Truly a small world, is it not?"

"Ah, so you are the mysterious young nephew that has taken Scotland Yard by storm? Yes, yes, Lady Cornelia has said she's most impressed since you've finished your training and come into your profession. Soon to be a detective, she assured me," Jaime replied.

He looked from Constable Weston to me and physically moved me so that I was standing next to Luke. I gave my cousin a quizzical brow and looked over at Constable Weston, who was doing the same.

"I must say cousin, it would almost appear as if you two have dressed to match!"

Luke and I looked at each other, our eyes lingering on the complementary elements of our dress, and both let out a laugh.

"Too true, Jaime, I think you are right!"

"Yes, indeed. A definite match for sure," Constable Weston said before catching my eye and holding it. We smiled a few moments too long before he cleared his throat.

Just then, the manticore came back, not carrying his usual pitcher of punch, and landed on my shoulder with leather-clad claws. No bigger than a small cat, I looked up at his whiskered face, and he began to purr in my ear. My cousin and Constable Weston had shocked looks on their faces, and I couldn't help but laugh.

"Apparently, I've made a friend," I said.

"A very smart manticore indeed, then," came a voice from behind me. I turned to find Miro, I mean, Mr. Nassar, standing there with a crooked smile.

"I can honestly say I've never seen him do that before. How

interesting," he continued. We chatted for a few more moments before we heard the tell-tale tuning up of instruments to indicate it was almost time to dance.

Constable Weston turned to me and said, "Would you care to dance, Miss Sweeting?"

Before I could reply, Mr. Nassar stepped forward and said, "I'm afraid she is spoken for on this first dance. I must be allowed to make amends for a previous misunderstanding. I am sure you understand, Mr....?"

"This is Mr. Luke Weston," I supplied. Constable Weston smiled as I said his name. "He is a nephew to Lady Whipley. He is also a brilliant constable on his way to becoming a detective, I understand."

"I thank you for that most kind introduction, milady. And since this first dance is spoken for, may I request the dinner waltz?" he asked. The dinner waltz was the longest dance, just before the meal, and also has the added benefit of allowing those partners to sit next to each other at the table. I blushed and nodded my head in acceptance at the request.

"Ah, yes well, it is nice to meet you, Mr. Weston. I must look to the papers in the future for any reference to your budding career. Let us make our way to the dance floor, Miss Annabelle," he said, offering me his arm. The manticore took his cue and flew off back to its duties. I took Miro's arm gingerly and was led out to the middle of the floor.

8

Chapter 8- Dance With Me

What do you mean your dance card is full? You must be joking.

Miro and I took our positions as the other couples made their way to join us. I took in the band. A young gentleman with sandy brown hair and a rather distinctive mustache played the galoubet. Another man in his late forties played a rose brass flute and wore a leather vest with beautiful embroidery. A third gentleman held his tambourine at the ready and wore a most fetching feather bowler hat.

The last member, an alluring young lady with the most gorgeous red hair I'd ever seen, was cradling her fiddle with reverence. The gypsy-like top and green leather skirt made her look like a wood nymph. Her eyes, a crystal blue, gleamed merriment as she scanned the floor at the crowd forming. Once the line formed, she took her bow and struck out the first notes with vigor. I almost missed my steps from the distraction of her.

Mr. Nassar and I moved well together, with almost machine-like precision. Although he was a most amiable partner, I couldn't help my eyes being drawn to the fiddle player. She was mesmerizing with her energy. I smiled sweetly at Miro in an attempt to cover up my distraction. When the song came to an end, we headed towards the edge of the room.

"Who is that most entertaining fiddler?" I inquired. "She is absolutely stunning."

"Ah yes, that is Miss Katherine Hayes. A gem from the Irish realm, for sure," he replied.

Jaime joined us then and introduced Lady Whipley to me. I found her quite regal, and she invited me to tea two days hence. During our conversations, a strew of young men came for introductions, and they asked me for space on my dance card. I looked to Jaime for guidance, and he provided one from his pocket with Luke Weston already scrawled upon it twice. He smiled conspiratorially at me. I found all the attention quite jarring.

A couple of bruised toes and several interesting conversations later, I found myself in the arms of Constable Weston for the dinner waltz. He positioned his hands with precision and led me around the dance floor with ease. We started out shy but soon were lost in conversation and the pace of the dance.

"So you want to become a world-renowned detective?" I started. "That sounds very exciting and full of mystery."

"Yes, but it also can be dull and full of paperwork," he quipped. "My mother's side have always had lawmen in the family, I guess you could say it's in the blood. As for detective, I just like solving puzzles, and to solve a puzzle of murder and mayhem – what could be more rewarding?" he said.

"Most honorable indeed," I said. "I have a very great fondness for justice, you see, and finding the truth in things. No matter how ugly, facts are what make this world reasonable. I also like to find the details in things. Like, take that gentleman over there, Mr. Canville. He claims to have stopped smoking a month ago. However, his mustache and his smudged thumb would suggest that to be untrue. Lady Valletta over there has been boasting about the natural blue roses her garden has provided for the centerpieces, but look at the blue dye beneath her fingernails as she removes her glove," I said.

"You do seem to have a very perceptive eye, Miss Sweeting. I wonder what you perceive about me?" he teased.

"Only that you either do not know how to sew, or haven't the time for it, you take walks in the Garden on Ives Street, and you share a fondness for lavender," I answered.

"And how did you come to these conclusions? I grant you the lavender, as we are both wearing it, but as for the other two?" he said.

"When we first met, you were wearing your constable uniform. The button second from the top and the one on your left wrist were loose. Suggesting one, that you were single and had no lady to mend them, and two, that you did not know how to mend them yourself. As someone who had very shiny boots, I knew that you took great pains with your appearance. As for the walks, well, the tops of your boots were quite shiny and polished but the bottoms had the reminiscences of a very distinct red-gray dirt that is found along the trail of that park near the fountain's edge. Your shoes tonight also have that dirt on them. Which, giving reason, would suggest you frequent there often," I finished.

He smiled at me then and pulled me in a fraction closer. "Quite remarkable you are, Miss Annabelle." I blushed at his use of my first name. He stared down at me, causing my breath to catch. "Interesting that my being single counted as number one on your observational list," he teased. I didn't think I could go another shade of red, but I am sure that's just what happened.

I blinked hard and looked around to break the intense moment, only to realize that the song was over and people were making their way to the dining area. Luke coughed to cover up the surprise he also experienced and offered his arm to me. I suddenly grew aware that I was no longer thinking of him as just Constable Weston. Accompanying this thought was a strange feeling of unease. Two other things I noticed were my cousin, Jaime, grinning slyly, and Mr. Nassar, scowling, both eyes pointed in my direction. Definite unease.

9

Chapter 9- Polite Conversation

This soup is divine. You, however, need some serious spicing up.

We entered the dining hall to the sound of many conversations fighting for dominance. Cheerful and spirited, the drone of words melded together. We stood behind our chairs on the far right corner and waited for Lord Thetford to begin the feast. The room quieted as he entered from the back doorway. Standing by the head of the table, his amber eyes scanned his guests. Sharp and focused, they hunted for something unknown to me. Miro stood by his chair just to the left, adjacent to Lord Thetford.

Jaime sat next to Lady Whipley and said something that sent her into a fit of giggles. He sat next to Lady Thetford, on Lord Thetford's right side. I turned back to see Lord Thetford staring at me, and a predatory smile spread across his face. I shivered at its intensity. He spoke and nodded to the couple just next to Miro, and they began a game of telephone and shuffling down. Those two chairs now stood open. When the shuffling reached Luke and me, we turned to find a servant beckoning us to follow him to the unoccupied seats by Miro. My stomach dropped at the proposition of sitting between these two gentlemen. Jaime stood directly across from me and could barely suppress his enjoyment at my tortured look.

Lord Thetford looked as we approached and said, "Now, isn't this better? Of course, we must make amends for our previous introduction, Miss Sweeting, and I understand we have a very promising constable in our midst." He turned to Lady Whipley and continued. "He is your nephew, is that correct, Cornelia? If he is so promising, we need to get him under the tutelage of Chief Inspector Farthing." He motioned his arms out and indicated we could all take our seats.

When she was seated, Lady Whipley replied. "Yes, Lord Thetford, he is my sister's son. I do believe his supervising officer is who you mentioned. Is it not so, Luke?"

She looked across to him for confirmation. Luke agreed with a nod of his head. The zooming of mechanical wings could be heard as the servants began distributing the first course.

My little friend, the manticore, and several others were lighting giant globe-like braisers surrounding the table. This earned a series of praise from the onlookers. A golden narwhal fluttered from soup to soup, distributing pepper when requested. I picked up my spoon with my left hand and accidentally bumped elbows with Luke. I smiled with a tinge of pink on my cheeks and apologized.

"I'm left-handed, Constable Weston. I fear we may bump elbows again," I said.

"I think I can brave your assault, Miss Sweeting," he winked.

My blush deepened. Miro cleared his throat with agitation, and I turned to see Lord Thetford smirking at him.

"Lord Thetford, I must compliment you on your most festive and beautiful party adornments. Quite splendid," I said, trying to break the weird tension.

"Miss Sweeting, you are too kind. I thank you. Yes, we try to put together a good show for our friends and investors. This is a little bit of business and pleasure, you see. We throw about three events a year and tend to gain a lot of our backing for our new inventions at them. Nothing like good food and beautiful women to dance with to get investors to open their purses, you know," he quipped.

"That is a very good practice. Are you working on anything new now?" I asked.

Miro turned to face me with excitement dancing in his peridot eyes. "We are working on something quite splendid, actually. We hope to debut it at the next event in a couple months. I won't ruin the surprise, but I can tell you that your little friend the manticore is a clue," he said.

As if on cue, the manticore swooped down and rested on the back of my chair. It let out the cutest little mechanical lion roar at Luke and then Miro, and leaned in to sniff the mechanized crown still fluttering on my head. I turned to face the creature's eyes, and it began to chuff affectionately.

"Are you giving your creations personalities?" I guessed. "This one seems to be fixated on me in a most protective manner."

Lord Thetford chuckled. "You could say that," he said.

"I think it's more of a specific trait we were going for within a personality," said Miro. "Affection, devotion, loyalty…" he trailed off. "Now that's all you get," he said, cutting me off before I could ask another question.

We continued chatting as the different courses came out. Some had many different flavors that I'd never experienced before. I was practically stuffed to the brim before I remembered that we still had the rest of the evening of dancing to contend with. I excused myself to the ladies' powder room, and my ever-watchful manticore trailed me.

As I entered, I turned to him and said, "you stay here and guard the entrance….what shall I call you? I think, Purgatorio. Perhaps you will lead me to Paradise as you did for Dante, no?" I quipped. He puffed out his chest and wings in agreement at the name. He then landed just outside the door and stood vigil as I went in.

10

Chapter 10- An Evening Well Spent

Spin me, dip me, do what you will...oh wait, decorum!

Entering the powder room, I found myself contemplating the intriguing invention the brothers were working on. A personalized mechanical companion, perhaps? Deep in thought, I didn't notice the entrance of the two ladies until I found their reflections crowding mine in the mirror. The Cosswalds stood on either side of me, and I almost giggled as they reminded me of an angel and devil on my shoulders. Or could they be two devils?

"Miss Sweeting, may I compliment you on your fine dancing?" said Miss Whitney. "It seems you have taken society quite by storm this evening!"

"I thank you for your kind words, Miss Cosswald, I had every intention of being an observer tonight, but it seems I was wrong. How are you enjoying this evening's festivities?" I asked.

"I think it's been a most exceedingly diverting evening and I can't wait for..."

"Whitney, enough of your prattling, we were hoping you would be so kind as to take tea with us Wednesday afternoon, Miss Sweeting,"

Miss Cara interrupted. "And be sure to extend our invitation to your cousin, Mr. Nethersby."

So, there was the catch. I knew the Miss Cosswalds were up to some sort of scheme, and befriending me in the directive of getting closer to my cousin was the soup du jour.

"Miss Cosswalds, I will relay your invitation to my cousin and see if he has time to spare from his demanding position with Lady Whipley. If not, I will surely be there," I said.

Despite looking disappointed, the ladies said thank you and left with their heads bent in conspiring conversation . I was not sure I wanted to further my acquaintance with them, but I knew it would be rude to not accept their invitation. If they turned out to be torturous companions, I would simply feign a headache and make my escape.

Walking outside the powder room, I was surprised to find Purgatorio still standing guard.

"Next time warn me if those harpies are about to descend," I chided.

He chuffed affectionately at me and took flight into the ballroom. I walked towards the refreshment table and found myself next to Miss Hayes, the lovely violinist.

"Miss Hayes, my name is Annabelle Sweeting, and I must tell you how extraordinary your playing has been this evening! You are truly gifted!" I exclaimed.

"Miss Sweeting, you are too kind. I am so happy to make your acquaintance," she replied. "I do love to play, and to know I am bringing joy to others is icing on the cake. I must return to my post now, as it seems the next set is to begin shortly." She seemed to float across the floor towards the band. Her red hair bounced as she went.

I sipped my lemonade and smiled. I scanned the room and found my distressed cousin trying to catch my eye. He was slowly being cornered by the Cosswald sisters and needed rescuing. I weaved towards him through the bustling couples getting ready for the next reel.

"Cousin Belle, you did not forget you promised me a dance?" He shouted as I approached. "Let us take the floor now. Sorry ladies, I am engaged to my fair cousin for the next dance," he said to the Cosswalds with such dramatic flair. Taking my hand in haste, we made our way out to a clear spot and waited for the band to begin. "You saved me in the nick of time, dear cousin. I thought they were going to put a sack over my head and whisk me away into the night," he jested.

"Jaime, they have invited us to tea next Wednesday, and I have accepted, but I gave you the option of being too busy at work to attend. I did not want to slight them by saying no outright, but if you think it unwise to become friendly with them, I will find an excuse to cancel," I replied.

"Dear cousin, they are a part of the upper crust and have many friends that could help you progress in society for sure, but their company is best in small doses. I would say keep the appointment and see what diversion can come of it. I always thought Miss Whitney to be much kinder than her sister, perhaps a friend may be worth seeking in her," he said.

"Thank you for your advice cousin, will you be joining me?"

"I think I would only prove to be a distraction. These girls, for some reason, have put me in their crosshairs, and I don't want to give them any unnecessary hope in that circumstance," he said. He twirled me around quickly, and then the music began to play, and I giggled as we dashed to catch up to the step.

The evening progressed deliciously, and we continued dancing to the lively band and the lovely nymph violinist. I danced with Lord Thetford once, and again with his brother Miro. Miro seemed to loosen up and be his more jovial self once the mingling with investors had finished. All the while, I could see Purgatorio circling above us as if he was a part of the dance. Miro followed my eye to the ceiling, where the manticore glided and grinned.

"Yes, I think that he has definitely attached himself to you. How peculiar," he observed.

"Purgatorio is quite the sky dancer, don't you think?" I quipped.

"Purgatorio? Oh, what an interesting name you've given him. Yes, I like that, indeed. If you would permit, I would like to lend him to you on a trial run."

Before I could protest, he continued, "you would be doing me a favor, I assure you. This is exactly the testing we need to verify our technology is working. Purgatorio, as you call him, is the first one inundated with the new prototype. I wasn't sure what to expect tonight, but he seems to have very good taste," he said with a wink.

Intrigued, I asked, "What exactly have you in mind for me to do with him?"

"I would like you to go about your day as usual, but give him tasks once in a while. And take him with you when you go out. What I want to know is, how he does following your instruction, and if you feel protected," he replied.

"Protected? Oh, I see, that is the goal, is it? Personal, mechanical bodyguards? Interesting, indeed."

"Please do keep your insights to yourself, Miss Sweeting, we don't want the masses knowing what we are up to just yet," he said. I nodded in understanding. We made our way to the side of the room where Lord and Lady Thetford were standing.

I curtsied politely to the lady and complimented her on the wonderful gathering.

"Yes, yes I suppose it is a fine affair, not that I worry about such things. I'm just glad no one had anything spilled on themselves by these hovering mechanical miscreants," she said, gesturing to the mythical creatures buzzing about the room.

"You do not like the lord's inventions then? I could see them being quite invasive. Although, these seem to be quite useful and beautiful at once," I said.

She inclined her head close to me and quietly said, "Sure they seem useful now, but you were not here for the previous models! I swear I've had at least five dresses ruined by their blunders!"

I snickered at her revelation, and the two gentlemen glanced at us in question. "With great advancement comes great sacrifice, Lady Thetford, but I'm sure in the end it will be wonderful for your family," I replied softly.

"Yes, I am sure you are right, and please call me Talia. I find you very easy to talk to, Miss Sweeting. Would you be opposed to meeting in town some time next week for tea or luncheon?" she asked.

"I would be delighted, Talia, and you must call me Annabelle. I am still quite new to the city, so if you could name the place I would be glad to meet you there at any time convenient," I said. We worked out the details to meet the following Thursday at a quaint diner that she assured me had the best pastries in the town.

As we ended our conversation, I felt a presence at my elbow and turned to find Luke peering down at me.

"Hello Lady Thetford, Miss Sweeting. I believe we have one last dance on the card," he said.

"Oh my goodness, I didn't mean to neglect you, Constable Weston."

I took his arm, and he led me to the floor. The first notes of the violinist soared, and our hands met in the middle. We spun in unison, never breaking eye contact. The haunting tones melded with the movements of the dance perfectly. We moved as if transfixed by some other force. His warm hand touched the small of my back as we made another turn. I glanced at his mouth, which had parted slightly, and thought how strong and yet soft it looked. And then he smirked. My eyes darted to his, and I flushed as his smile broadened. It felt like only seconds had passed, and then the song ended.

I shook my head clear as I looked around the room. Luke guided me to my cousin's side and politely took his leave, looking a bit lost himself.

I don't think I've ever enjoyed a dance more.

11

Chapter 11- Unsavory Developments

Is it the most foul or fabulous things that happen in the shadows? Jury still out.

I woke early with a lightness I couldn't quite comprehend. I put on a dark blue dress with a half skirt. I cinched it in the middle with a dark leather corset. My pantaloons were a lighter tan material and had several hidden pockets in the ruffles just below the knees, and I wore calf-high boots with half-moon buckles up the side and a slim zipper pouch on the toes. My newest hat depicted a brass and iron daisy pattern with vines around the band. Tiny bees fluttered on the flora with spring-action wings. I thought of my bouquet brooch, and a pang of longing hit me. It would have complimented the hat perfectly. I completed the ensemble with the leather rucksack Charles Kaplan had given me, embellished with royal blue trim and rose brass buckles.

I walked down the stairs and found Nathan waiting for me at the bottom. He held a large parcel in his hands and approached me quickly.

"This came for you miss, it's pretty heavy! I think it's from that cabbie guy at the pawty," he said. I opened it quickly and found Purgatorio resting inside. The note read,

Miss Sweeting,

Please find Purgatorio safely inside. Just press his nose 3 times to wake him up.

Thank you again for participating in our little experiment. The manticore will recharge himself when needed. If there is a malfunction and you need immediate shut-off, use the word Catacomb. I will reach out to you in a week to see how things are progressing. Please send a card to the below address if you need help before then.

Your Servant,
Honourable Miro Nassar
425 Thetford Tower, London E3 FHU

I had forgotten all about the mechanical manticore and now felt guilty. I unwrapped Purgatorio quickly and clicked his lion nose three times.

He sputtered to life and opened his maw in a yawn. Blinking his eyes towards me, a glint of recognition followed by a series of clicks led to him taking flight and landing on my shoulder. Nathan stood in awe at the mechanical myth and took a step forward. Purgatorio directed a warning roar toward him, and I admonished him directly.

"Purgatorio, Nathan is my friend. You will treat him in the same manner you treat me or you will go back in the box. Understood?"

He chuffed once in response and sidled up beside Nathan in apology. Nathan stroked his smooth brass mane with wonder.

"Be careful of his tail Nate, those spikes look sharp," I warned.

"Yes missus, shall we be takin' him with us this mornin' then?" He asked,

"Actually, I need you to take this missive to Lady Thetford, and I will meet you at the glass shop afterward. I haven't purchased the lenses for the blacksmith yet, and I wanted to get those done before we visit him this week. I will be taking a morning stroll by myself today," I said.

"You sure you want to do that, missus? I can go with ya," he said.

"It is fine Nathan, I will take Purgatorio with and if I run into any mishap he will come find help, does that suit?"

I could tell he wanted to protest more but nodded his head instead. We departed before the sun rose, snatching two scones each from the tray as we headed out the door. I walked along the street with no real destination. I was used to taking these strolls back home and missed the freedom and ideas these walks provided me.

The manticore took flight above me and soared above the buildings never, straying out of the line of sight. I watched as the stores I passed started to prepare themselves for the day. They were sweeping the sidewalks, shining up the windows and doorknobs, and changing up the displays in the windows. The smells from the bakery were already making my mouth water, and I quickly took a bite of one of my scones. A sense of calm washed over me as the opening sounds of the city began to ring out. They were like an orchestra's first notes.

I wandered on for about a mile before I realized I wasn't too far from the Garden at St. Ives Street. It was a beautiful prospect, with different varieties of rose bushes, massive oaks, and a fountain in the center depicting a scene from *Shakespeare's Midsummer Night's Dream*. A satyr with a lute pranced around a rocky feature, while two pairs of lovers slumbered under a fairies' tree on the lower tier. The tree branches reached skyward and swept down like a willow. The water, spurting from the different spots along the limbs, created a magical display. It almost looked like the water produced more branches. I started walking in that direction when I heard my name called from behind me.

"Miss Sweeting, I thought that was you," Constable Weston said. "What are you doing out so early this morning?" He was dressed in his uniform and appeared to be heading in the same direction. "Are you alone, as well?" He asked.

"Constable Weston! What a surprise. I was taking a morning walk to clear my mind and found myself being pulled toward the garden. Purgatorio is above keeping vigil, as you see, so I am not quite alone," I said. He peered up to see the manticore descending in response to his presence and stepped closer to me in reflex.

"That is quite the beastie. I doubt anyone would approach you if they saw that thing close at hand," Luke said.

I waved to Purgatorio to show him I was fine, and he continued his circular flying pattern as we walked.

"Constable Weston, are you heading to the garden as well? Is it part of your route?" I inquired.

I watched him make a face as if he'd been caught stealing cookies. "I am actually due at the Yard shortly, but I think I have a little time to spare," he admitted.

He took my arm and placed it on the inside of his forearm. His face still clouded in the morning shadow, was calm and content. We walked comfortably toward the garden's entrance and through its stone arches. I watched the birds and squirrels scurry through the trees as they began their day. The twilight of the morning faded, and the light flickered through the leaves.

Walking towards the garden's center, we came to where the trail changed from gravel to red-gray dirt. It laced along and around the fountain ahead. As we approached the pool, the sun started to shine down, spreading light throughout the park. Looking towards the far left edge of the fountain, I noticed the dirt was darker red.

At first, I thought it was a trick of the light as the sun rose. My second thought was that the fountain was leaking water and had dampened the dirt, but the color wasn't quite right. I started to lead Luke towards the left, and he paused for a moment.

"What is it, Miss Annabelle? You seem distressed all of a sudden," he said.

"Luke, I have a bad feeling that when we turn that corner, our morning will no longer be content," I whispered.

His eyes followed to where I was indicating, and we proceeded to walk in that direction. We rounded the fountain, and I gasped.

We saw in front of us the bloodied body of the beautiful, violin-playing wood nymph.

12

Chapter 12- A Surprising Bouquet

"My course is set for an uncharted sea." - Dante Alighieri

Katherine Hayes, the lovely violinist from the previous night, was now perched upon the stone branches of the fountain at the Garden at St. Ives Street. Her limbs were positioned as if she were dancing across the water. Her glazed, dead eyes stared up toward the east, where she would never again see the sunrise. Katherine's once beautiful dress was destroyed by the blood released from a dreadful wound upon her neck. As I stood there in horror, Luke began to list off tasks we needed to do. He did not want to leave the scene unguarded, but we had to get word to his superior, Chief Inspector Farthing. Luke took out his notepad and started jotting down things and placing them around the scene. He secured them with a pebble as he positioned them by items of importance.

I raised my fingers to my lips and let out a shrill whistle, as little Nathan had taught me. Luke gave me a startled look but then continued at his task. Now, realizing where my morning had led me, I wished I had taken Nathan's offer of accompanying me. Then again, I was glad he was not here to witness this shocking scene.

Purgatorio dove down towards us and landed on the edge of the trail. His spiked tail was arched above his head, and wings spread with menace as he surveyed the scene.

"Purgatorio, we need your help, calm yourself," I directed.

"Luke, give me a piece of that paper, please, and your pencil," I said.

I wrote down the location on a cryptic yet forceful note directing the chief inspector to come quickly. Beckoning the manticore to me, I instructed him to take the rolled-up parchment to the building with the people dressed just like Luke. I waited for him to affirm that he had seen my description of Scotland Yard from his circling dance through the sky.

"Luke, what does Chief Inspector Farthing look like? Anything distinguishable?"

"Yes, he has a rather large mustache that curls up at the ends," he replied absently. Luke's mind was still invested in jotting down details of the gruesome scene before us.

"You hear that, Purgatorio?" He chuffed in response. He rubbed his metallic mane in my hand before he took flight towards Scotland Yard.

We waited about a half-hour before the chief inspector made his way to the Garden on St. Ives Street.

He brought several officers with him and began directing them to guard the perimeters of the garden so no other passersby would happen upon the spot. He walked towards us with a slight limp in his right leg and a stern look. I saw Purgatorio walking behind him with his tail up menacingly. It was as if he was trying to urge him forward faster.

"Constable Weston! Is this horrid creature yours? I want an explanation why you would summon me with no more than a cryptic note saying you need bodies here post-haste and this creature chasing me about," he demanded.

Luke looked pale as he registered that I had summoned his superior officer with so little decorum.

"Chief Inspector Farthing, I fear the fault is mine," I interjected. "My name is Annabelle Sweeting, and the manticore is mine.

Purgatorio, please leave the chief inspector to do his job, and stop being rude." Purgatorio let out a chuff and walked away from the Inspector. He trotted up to my side and sat stoically. "Chief Inspector, I did not want to go into details in the note in case Purgatorio got lost and delivered it to the wrong person. However, if you come over here, I think the scene will help to clarify the urgency."

He made his way over to us and slowly rounded the fountain. A flicker of surprise registered on his face but was gone the next instant. He looked at the ground where pieces of paper marked the blood pool, some footprints, and a few bits of rubbish. He looked back up at the poor girl and studied her more closely; then, turned towards us once again.

"Chief Inspector, I apologize for the method in which we retrieved your attention, but I did not want to leave the scene in case anything were to be disturbed," Luke said.

"Yes, yes, very well. I see that you have plotted out some findings already, Constable Weston, is it?"

"Yes, sir."

"This looks like a fine job so far, and since you are keen to become a detective, you will continue to assist me with this one, understood?"

"Yes, sir!"

"Now, as for you, Miss Sweeting, I'm surprised you are not swooning away. You seem to have some mettle to you. Just keep that horrid beast away from me," he said.

Purgatorio hissed.

"Yes, Chief Inspector. I will work on training him up on his manners, sir. Also, we did not want to touch anything until you got here, but I noticed her hands were clenched shut. One seems to be holding a tear of paper and the other something metallic," I said.

Chief Inspector Farthing and Luke advanced closer to the body to peer at the hands. They were leaning over the very edge of the fountain before they both gasped with the affirmative.

"Miss Sweeting, how did you see that from back there? I had not noticed that at all," Luke said. He looked somewhat sullen at having missed a vital clue.

"I told you, Constable Weston, I have a knack for details, " I replied.

Chief Inspector Farthing ignored us and took out a pocket knife. He turned it open and used the flat edge to slowly pry open one hand. He grasped tweezers from his inside pocket and released the piece of paper from her right hand.

Luke and I edged closed to see what was written.

The paper was no more than two inches wide by two inches tall. It looked ripped from a book and had an edge of an ink-printed etching on it. A jagged "T" was written in the corner, and what could be deciphered from the picture was a hill with a cave entrance and stairs carved into the cave going downward. The rest of the image was cut off.

Farthing folded it carefully in a handkerchief and handed it to Luke. He returned to the body and did the same process on the left hand. As he spun around to show us the metallic object, I audibly gasped. Laying on a once pristine white handkerchief in his hand was a blood-stained brooch. The flower petal gears were now caked with dried blood and twitching with excursion as they tried to spin. I looked up at the violinist's face. Why did Katherine Hayes have my brooch clutched in her cold dead hand?

13

Chapter 13- Suspects, Suspects Everywhere

All things are fair in love and war, but what of espionage?

I couldn't wrap my head around the fact that Katherine Hayes had my brooch in her hand. My mind was blanking for the first time I could remember, and I fought myself for control. I needed to focus on the facts. Shaking my head forcibly, I found Chief Inspector Farthing and Constable Weston staring at me with concern. *Had they said something?*

I reminded myself that I had more sense than this and straightened my stance. The best thing to do was not to panic and jump to conclusions when trouble was afoot.

"Gentlemen, I apologize. Did you ask me something?"

"Miss Sweeting, we were just inquiring about your health, you seemed quite on the verge of hysterics a moment ago," said Farthing. "Does this piece of jewelry mean something to you, that it invoked such a reaction?"

"As a matter of fact, Chief Inspector, it does. Up until about a fortnight ago, that brooch belonged to me," I replied.

The Inspector looked at me in question. His eyes assessed me in an effort to cipher out my role in the demise of this young lady.

Luke stepped closer to me and took my hand. The slightest tremor shivered through my body.

He looked at his superior and said, "Chief Inspector, I trust this lady, and before we jump to unjust conclusions, let us hear her out."

Farthing nodded his agreement. "Miss Annabelle, please tell us what you know about this bauble."

I was innocent, so why was I acting guilty? Perhaps it was the initial shock, but something snapped, and I clawed my way back to being rational. Looking into Luke's reassuring eyes, I plunged forward into my story of One-eyed Whitmore and the trade for the dagger cuff. I displayed the thick bracelet along my wrist as I described the interaction. As I told the story, I thought, if I had heard it from someone else I would think they were making it all up. Farthing was hard to read, he scrutinized me closely while I continued.

Luke nodded his head as I spoke, never showing an ounce of skepticism. I don't know why, but I left out the part that my cousin, Jaime, had been searching for Whitmore these past few days in hopes of trading to get the brooch back. Perhaps, I didn't want him in the cross hairs that I currently felt ensnared in. Once I completed my story, Chief Inspector Farthing called the nearest officer. He told the officer to gather a couple more men from the Yard and search for One-eyed Whitmore. The officer shuddered at the name and made the sign of the cross upon his chest. He hurried off before anything more could be asked of him.

Chief Inspector Farthing gave Luke and me an assessing look and said, "My instincts tell me you are not responsible Miss Sweeting, but my post demands me to say don't leave town. Understood?"

I nodded my head in agreement.

"Chief Inspector, I would like to help in any way I can to clear myself of any suspicion. I would not have pointed out the brooch in her hand if I had been the one to place it there. I would like to offer my observational assistance to Constable Weston if possible. I do not like that someone has tried to tie me to this heinous crime. Please, sir?"

"We are rather stretched thin, but I don't see a woman handling this gruesome work. However, you did have the presence of mind to notify me with some subtlety, and you noticed several key clues quicker than both Constable Weston and I." He continued to think out loud. "You also are clearly smart enough to not leave incriminating evidence to pin on yourself. Plus, if you are the culprit, Constable Weston will be right there to apprehend you if need be, or keep you safe from the real killer." He chuckled menacingly at that.

"I don't like the idea of a civilian coming in on this, let alone a woman. But, I feel in this case, with you being immediately implicated, the killer is looking to keep you involved in some way. If you're willing to help, all the better, as we would want to keep you close either way."

He turned to Luke and said, "Constable Weston you will need to keep me up to date on any findings. I will need to talk to our superiors and get their input on how to address the press. I will hold you personally responsible for any trouble Miss Sweeting gets into, understood? " He concluded.

Luke looked at me with a slight smile and agreed.

With a curt nod to each of us, Chief Inspector Farthing turned away and directed his officers to wrap up the scene.

Luke took me off to the side while the team took the body down and prepared it for transport back to the morgue. It was sad that such a vibrant light had been snuffed out so swiftly and brutally. I had all but forgotten Purgatorio when his screech and the sound of an irate Nathan Starling hit my ears. Looking toward the entrance, I could see Nate arguing with the guarding officer to let him through. Purgatorio threatened with his spike-laced tail.

Releasing Luke's hand, I dashed over to the confrontation. Nathan took one look at me and launched himself into my arms.

"Missus, missus, I heard such terrible reports! They was saying a lady was dead cawld, they was. I just knew they was lying!" He squeezed me tighter.

"Nathan, calm yourself, I am fine. Purgatorio was ever in eyesight until he went in search of you just now." I stroked his head gently. "Yes, there was a woman killed, but it was not me."

He shuddered and looked up into my eyes with tear-soaked ones of his own. Purgatorio circled our legs and purred.

"Missus, I am ne'er lettin' you ditch me again." It sounded like a vow, and I hugged him in reassurance. We headed out of the guarded area, and I looked back at Luke. He finished with his notes and moved to follow Katherine to the morgue. He looked up at me and jogged over. We continued to walk toward the entrance of the park.

"Miss Sweeting, I might have a few more questions regarding the brooch, would it be okay if I called on you tomorrow?"

"Yes, Constable Weston. Don't you want me to come with you now?" I replied.

He was just about to say something else when a familiar motor came barreling down the lane on St. Ives Street. It screeched to a halt outside the entrance, and Miro jumped out, rushing towards us.

"Miss Sweeting, I am glad to see you safe!" He exclaimed.

"Yes, I am quite safe, Mr. Nassar. Why are you in such a state, and how did you know I would be here?"

His eyes glanced at Purgatorio and then back to me. His face flushed with guilt or embarrassment; I wasn't sure which. Then, I turned to Purgatorio and looked more closely. His left eye was no longer red, but black and reflective like a mirror or a lens. Crouching down, I looked into the eye and back at Miro.

"Is this what I think it is?"

"Miss Sweeting, I can explain, I was merely testing the functionality of the visual receptor, and when I saw the shocking scene I dashed immediately here to make sure you were okay," he blurted.

"Mr. Nassar, are you telling me that you've installed a visual spying device on a prototype that you have requested me to assess, and didn't tell me? Are you also stating that had I been anywhere else, let's say, my bed chambers or speaking privately with a friend, that you could "have happened" to be testing the functionality then as well?" My face was heating up with the anger swelling in me.

"Now that you say it out loud, I can see that I have erred and offended you; that was not my intent. I hadn't even thought about those scenarios, I assure you. I only thought that you would be out in town at this time of day, and I wanted to see how the prototype was keeping up. I will deactivate the link right now, " he said.

He bent down and unscrewed a bolt by the side of Purgatorio's eye, removed a chip, and closed the bolt. The eye returned to its fiery red hue. It was almost the same as my flushed face.

Luke stepped towards Miro with menace.

"Sir, I think it best that you take your beast and leave Miss Sweeting alone," he stated. Then turned to me, "Miss Sweeting, I think you should head home and rest. This has been a very trying day, and I will need you at your best tomorrow if we are to hit this case full force. The examiner won't be in until first light to look at the body; he was out in the borough all day."

"I'll take her home," said Miro. "I must make amends! I can tell you of all his features so there are no mistakes in the future. Also, was he not a great help today?" He pleaded to me with the feelings of an inventor. Purgatorio edged up to me, his eyes searching mine to detect if he had done something wrong.

Luke started, "I said to get…"

"Constable Weston, I will handle this," I interjected. "Mr. Nassar, I understand the importance of your work, and I must not deny Purgatorio was a real lifesaver today. But if another omission, a falsehood breaches your lips, I will wash my hands of this experiment and your acquaintance. Do I make myself clear, sir?"

Little Nate stood to my left and added, "And I'll kick ya right good in the shin, too!"

Purgatorio took a flank on my right and hissed at Miro with his tail raised.

"You see, he is more yours than mine now anyway!" Miro exclaimed as he pointed to the manticore.

Luke raised an eyebrow at me but could see my decision was made. He gave me a nod, although I knew he was unhappy with my choice to continue working with Miro. For some reason, I felt I needed Purgatorio.

"I agree to your terms, Miss Sweeting, and will strive to go above and beyond your expectations for redemption! Please, let me escort you and young Starling home as a first step," Miro said.

I turned to Luke and confirmed our meeting time on the morrow. Nathan and I followed Miro to his motor car and packed ourselves in. Before he could take off from the curb, I directed him to the glass shop. Murder was not going to stop me from my objective for the day. I needed to finish those goggles for the blacksmith.

14

Chapter 14- Down the Rabbit Hole

Each clue leads to a bigger question, are the stars against me, I wonder?

Miro steered the motor towards town, and we braced ourselves as he took the corners sharply. I sat in the front seat this time. Purgatorio rested between Miro and I. Nate leaned forward between the front seats from the back and peered out the front window.

Miro glanced at me several times as we raced down the side streets, dodging other motors and pedestrians. I left my icy wall erect. He would have to do much more than drive me about town to make up for his omission. We were there in no time, and Miro parked with a squeal. He jumped out and had his hand on my door before I could reach the handle.

"Allow me," he said. His peridot eyes searched mine for any sign of thawing.

We walked towards the glass shop. On the way in, Purgatorio let out a harsh chirp. He went to the side of the door and abruptly powered down. I looked at Miro in question.

"Ah, he needs to recharge. You will hear his gears whirling now as he powers his energy chamber. It shouldn't take long, but he looks to have given you a warning not to do anything exciting without him," Miro explained.

I laughed a little at that, and Miro smiled. The tension started to ease, just slightly, between us. We entered the shop, and I explored the different lenses. I had narrowed it down to several shades of blues and purples for the goggles I intended to make Charles the blacksmith. A smile spread across my face as I remembered that I had promised to bring Jaime with me when I delivered them to the rugged but handsome smithy.

"Oh, no! Jaime!" I shouted. The others turned to me, startled.

"Nathan, do you know if anyone informed my cousin of this morning's events? The shock of it all swept me up so completely that I forgot to communicate my safety," I said.

"No, missus. That is, I came from 'cross town, you see, after I delivered your missuve to the Lady T. That's when I heard the rumblings of the dead lady. I ran when I spotted Purgy, as he was causing a screechy racket in the sky. I just followed him, missus, as he was to be with ya," he explained.

"I need you to run and relay that I am fine to Jaime, in case he hears some altered tale of events. I was due to be home several hours ago," I said.

"Well, I'm nawt goin' anywheres, missus. I told ya I ain't leaving and that's that." Nathan stomped his foot for emphasis.

"I will take the message to him, Miss Sweeting," Miro jumped in. "I'll take the motor and be back in a flash. Don't leave the store until my return, okay? I will escort you home afterward?" He looked at me for confirmation.

"Yes, yes. Very well, Mr. Nassar. Please, relay my regard to my cousin, and let him know I will be home directly as soon as I procure the items for the blacksmith's goggles," I said.

He took off like a shot and jumped into the motor. Racing down the street at such a pace, you'd think there was a fire. I looked at Nate, and he had his arms crossed and face set, scrutinizing the other patrons of the glass shop with suspicion. I didn't realize how fast he had grown to claim the role as my little protector. I tried to contain a chuckle as I pictured him kicking grown men in the shins if they stepped out of line. Nate heard me and looked up in question. I shrugged my shoulders and raised my brows in jest. He shook his little determined head, walking around the store to scout the perimeter.

I turned back to the task at hand and rummaged through several bins of lenses before I settled on a pair of a deep lavender hue. They were enough to shade his eyes from the intense flames of the furnace, and light enough he could see the fine details of his work. The vendor drilled two small holes on the bottom left and right corners for the wiper blades I planned to insert. I would attach each side with a durable leather flap to block the side light. I chose a very hard lacquered wood frame to withstand the heat and not warm his face. They would secure to his head with an adjustable leather belting mechanism in the back. I hoped Charles would like them. The goggles were wrapped up carefully, and Nathan and I started to leave the shop. I was so deep in thought, breaking down the assembly of the glasses in my head, that I forgot to wait for Mr. Nassar's return.

The chuff at the side of the door alerted me to Purgatorio's recharged status. I looked down and smiled at him and watched him circle our legs. He trotted alongside us like a majestic house cat with deadly appendages. Turning towards the sidewalk that would lead back to Bread Street, I saw from the corner of my eyes a fleeing form. It rounded the alley between this shop and the next. My heart skipped a beat at the recognition I felt. I could have sworn I'd just seen One-eyed Whitmore. Also, I'm pretty sure he meant for me to see him. Before either the manticore or Nathan could stop me, I took off after him.

My heart raced as my feet pounded on the narrow brick alleyway.

I could hear Nathan running and shouting behind me as Purgatorio took to the sky to catch up. I was too fast for either of them. I dashed through the alley and dodged boxes and debris that littered my path. My hard-soled boots tapped out an accelerated beat on the bricked pavement below me. I ran with a need for redemption, and only One-eyed Whitmore could give it to me. I knew it was dangerous to confront him, but I had to know how it happened. I had to know. Why would he give me a dagger cuff to protect myself, only to frame me for murder?

I reached the end of the alley and turned left in the direction of a shadow I saw on the opposite wall. I rounded the corner and stumbled to a halt, almost running directly into One-eyed Whitmore's barreled chest. He took my shoulders and shook me with desperation. The shock and disbelief on his face were jarring. I could only hope I hadn't run myself right into the arms of a murderer!

"You've got to help me, miss," he started. " There are strange murmurings in the Brass Boroughs. They claim I've done a young miss in, but I haven't, I swear it. I'm being chased myself, by a demon! A haunting figure with a cloak and the tiniest bells to let you know you're done for. It's been looking for something, I don't know what, but I think the demon thinks I have it," he yelled.

His one good eye darted here and there, never really focusing on my face. Shadowed in despair, he took my hands in his.

"Miss, I swear it, I only aim to protect, never hurt no one."

"Mr. Whitmore, I don't know what you're saying about demons, but I know they found the brooch I traded you for in the young lady's hand where she died. How did it get there? Did you give it to her?"

"No, Miss Sweeting, no..." He looked at me directly with his pleading eye and took in what I had asked.

"The brooch, you see, I gave it to your cousin, Mr. Jaime Nethersby. He said you missed it so, and he traded me this fine leather bag for it."

Just then, Nathan came charging around the corner. One-eyed

Whitmore saw him and bolted. Purgatorio tried to dive bomb him from above, but once Whitmore turned down several more alleys, he gave up the chase. I stood awestruck. The words he spoke finally registered. My dear cousin, Jaime, had my brooch last? How could this be? There is no way he could have hurt someone, let alone murder. I needed to talk to him immediately before any bobbies got wind of his potential involvement.

15

Chapter 15- Sunshine and Secrets

When in peril of being too serious, look to family. There is sure to be some diversion afoot!

Nathan, Purgatorio, and I rounded the corner on Bread Street and headed for home. As we came into view of the front door, a startled Miro turned back towards us with wide eyes. He raced towards us and met us at the end of the walk.

"Miss Sweeting, I thought you were to wait for me? I was just about to head back that way to pick you up. Your cousin has been thoroughly appeased, I assure you. I had hoped to make amends on the way back," he said exasperated. I don't know why he thought he could fix things in one quick afternoon, but I appreciated his fervor about trying to atone for his bad judgment.

"Mr. Nassar, I thank you for your assistance today, and as you can see Purgatorio and Nathan were able to see me home. I will be out tomorrow morning on business, but I am to take afternoon tea with your sister-in-law, Lady Thetford. Perhaps, you can escort me home afterwards?"

Miro agreed and smiled in relief. He saluted to Nathan and ran

66

towards his motor to leave. " I'll see you tomorrow, then," he shouted out his window and was gone.

For some reason I felt like I was making it easy on him, but something about him made it hard to stay mad. Maybe it was the earnest way he pressed to make amends, or the genuine way he seemed distressed by my unhappiness. Or it could also be the sparkle in those green eyes that brightened when the anger subsided between us. I knew then that I would forgive him, but I must be on my guard around him. Fool me once and all that follows weighed heavily on my mind.

Right now, however, I needed to address a more important topic with my dear cousin, Jaime. I climbed several steps at once and before I could open the door, Stewart swung open the door and hurried me inside. Most unladylike, I know, but dire times call for dire actions.

The butler's outfit, somewhat toned down from the first arrival, still flared with the eccentric. A forest green ensemble with a black waistcoat was drawn together with a top hat of similar colors. The top hat had a pattern of what I thought were racing horses, and it was confirmed when the same embellishment was depicted on his sleeves. A little brass horse attached to his necktie had spring legs and gave the appearance of movement. This was definitely one of Jaime's better works. I ran past Stewart and to the front parlor, where I knew Jaime would be waiting for me.

Entering the parlor, I turned to Nathan and told him to have the maid prepare my room and directed him to eat something. I looked around the room for any other servants and closed the door promptly. Purgatorio protested so loudly that I gave in and let him in the room. Turning to my cousin, I saw the confusion on his face.

"Cousin Belle, what do you have to tell me so secretly?" He asked with a broad smile widening on his face. "Has some handsome beau stolen a kiss, and you're here to spill all the juicy details?" I looked at him for a moment and started laughing at his wiggling eyebrows.

"Ah, there she is, my beautiful cousin. I don't like to see your face marred with such serious expressions. I heard about today, my dear, and I am truly sorry you had to see such a thing. I am glad such an event hasn't stolen your sunshine completely."

"Jaime, I do need to talk to you about something most urgent and serious. I assure you, after this morning's fright, I am quite well. I am actually planning to assist Constable Weston tomorrow with the investigation."

"What? No, no. Assist in a murder investigation? Well, now that you say that, I can see you being quite a good sleuth. You were always finding clues to the unsolvable mishaps in the country. Like, when that ham of a boy, Walter Conray, was feeding the goats those wild onions and making their milk sour. Now that was quite the mystery until you saw all the seedlings growing in their pasture. The boy was in huge trouble for weeks." He laughed heartily at the memory.

"Yes, he was quite the little rascal, but cousin, you are derailing me from my pressing question." I smiled at him with true affection, then frowned with the concern I felt for the question I needed to ask.

"Yes, then dear, yes, ask me now before that expression becomes permanent!"

"Jaime, were you able to get the brooch back from One-eyed Whitmore that I traded for this cuff?"

"Is that all, Belle? That doesn't seem dire at all. I did actually get it back for you, and I meant to give it to you before the party," he stopped, face crestfallen. "However, I had the brooch in my pocket when I went to the party, and I forgot to give it to you with the onslaught of the Cosswalds. I handed my jacket to the attendant at the party, and when we arrived home later, I realized it was gone. I am so sorry, Belle. I have inquired with Lord and Lady Thetford to see if any of their help had come across it, but nothing has been found yet. Do you hate me?"

"Oh cousin, I could never hate you. To be truthful, I am exceedingly relieved at this turn of events. You see, cousin, the brooch has been found."

"What, where? Oh, I'm glad for you," he said.

"You won't be so glad when you hear this next part." He edged closer on his seat in anticipation. "The brooch was found with the dead violinist this morning."

The shock on Jaime's face was palpable. I thought he was going to fall down. He turned so pale, then he spoke once more.

"Oh Belle, what can this mean? This is quite frightful, indeed! Why would someone take it from my pocket and then leave it at a murder scene? You will be careful investigating this, won't you? I feel uneasy with this brooch so closely tied to you. Or, maybe," he said brightly. "The young lady took it herself and happened to accidentally die with it?" He shook his head, knowing that was not likely.

"Jaime, I assure you I will be careful, and I'll be with Purgatorio and Constable Weston, so there's no need to be uneasy." I said the words as much to myself as to him.

"So, Constable Weston will be accompanying you, will he? How convenient, I mean reassuring?" He said as I swatted his arm. "Yes, I see there is some pleasure in all this tragedy. Well, keep close and tell me all the details. Not, of the investigation of course, but of this budding new conquest of yours. We must not let the shade of death darken the brilliance of life, my dear Belle. Not one ounce!"

Just then, a knock came from the parlor door, and a servant entered with a missive for Jaime. He walked over to Jaime and placed it in his outstretched hand. Jaime waited until the servant had closed the door on his way out before opening the letter.

"It's from Lady Thetford; she states that she has inquired to her staff regarding the brooch and has come up empty handed. She does, however, reveal that her coat attendant noticed several amorous events in the closet and she will go into more detail with us tomorrow at tea?

Oh, are we going to tea?"

"Yes, dear cousin. I thought it would just be Lady Talia and I, but it appears she has included you into the invitation. I daresay the conversation will be diverting!"

"Belle, you brash little thing! That is something I would say." He started to chuckle at my blush. "Yes, I think it will be a most delightful afternoon."

16

Chapter 16- Morgue Morning

There is nothing quite like mixing romance and formaldehyde. An acquired taste, perhaps?

Upon waking up this morning, I felt wonderful. I was fully rested and happy to see the sunshine through my garden view window. That was the first ten seconds or so, then the previous day's events hit me. The shock of Katherine's perfectly posed, frightful body, the discovery of Miro's snooping mechanic lens, and the startling run-in with One-eyed Whitmore rushed through my system.

The anxiety of so much activity in such a short time was traumatizing. Then the thoughts of Luke's reassuring face, saying he trusted me, popped in. It helped put a balm on my nerves. A chuckle actually left my lips as the conversation with my dear cousin, Jaime, teasing me with wiggling eyebrows, wafted through my mind. Yes, there could be a lightness of heart, even in the darkest of times; you just had to be ready to accept it.

After a light breakfast, Nathan, Purgy, as Nate had started calling him, and I prepared to leave to meet the constable. When we stepped outside, Luke was waiting for us on the sidewalk.

"Bringing the whole party, I see?" He quipped. His deep brown eyes, red-rimmed with lack of sleep, were still heated with intensity.

"Constable Weston, it is nice to see you, sir. After yesterday's events, these two are most adamant about keeping a close watch. I haven't the heart to turn down such loyal and brave protectors, would you?" I smiled and looked up at him through my eyelashes.

"I daresay not, Miss Sweeting, such soldiers are rare, indeed." The upturn of his lips was just noticeable to me from this angle.

Nathan puffed up his chest.

"Ya got that right, constable, sir! I ain't leavin the missus for nawt a thing. Unless I need to use the privy, of course, but that will be lightning fast, I swear it!"

"I can well believe it, Mr. Starling. You will, however, need to remain outside the morgue while we conduct the examination. I am afraid only Miss Sweeting will have access as an appointed consultant," Luke said.

"I've seen enough bloaters in my time, no need for any more of that. I can wait outside, sir."

"Nathan! What a horrible way to reference the dead," I said. "Please find another, kinder word for it in my presence."

"Yes, missus. I apologize. How 'bout dearly departed? I've heard that used tons of times at them dirt digging parties at the cemetery."

"Yes, Nate. Dearly departed will do just fine," I said. There was no point in admonishing him further for fear of what new disturbing term he would invent next.

I shook my head a little, thinking about all this young man had seen before he came to me. It felt like we had been a team forever, but he had clearly gone through a lot before we met. I had seen improvements in his manners every day we spent together. Even his words were coming out more polished. Then he would get onto one of these subjects, and all polish flew out the window. Still, I wouldn't change him for anything. I hope he knew I liked his authentic style and valued the hardships he went through. Those experiences made him a strong ally, but they also made him my friend.

We reached the morgue. Nathan and Purgy stood outside either side of the double doors as I followed Luke through to the examination area. He introduced me to Doctor Cannish, the coroner, and we were instructed to stand aside while he prepared the area. The doctor was very meticulous in his arrangement of instruments and notes. The body remained covered until he had every item in its proper place.

"We are ready to proceed. Please do not faint in my exam room, I have no time for such distractions." His words were clipped and directed towards me.

"I wouldn't dream of it, doctor. Do continue. You need not worry on my account."

"Humph. We shall see." He slowly slid back the white sheet covering Katherine. I remained stoic as I already knew what was to be revealed. He peered up to me to see if I would swoon like the damsel he saw me as. I stared back at him in challenge. He raised his eyebrows at my directness and proceeded with the exam.

"Yes, well I can see she's been dead for at least a day and a half. Obviously, since you found her yesterday morning. Plus the rigor is quite pronounced now. I see my assistant has already taken the liberty of cleaning her up a bit, but rest assured his notes of her arrival are very thorough. Her neck has been sliced quite clean at the beginning but jagged toward the end. Looks like a left-handed person, with either not a lot of strength or maybe a dulling weapon." He used his forceps to spread the wound further. He jotted down some notes and continued moving down the body.

"Multiple contusions and cuts along the arms and abdomen. The abdomen seems a bit pronounced for this stage of decay. Perhaps internal bleeding? I will have to cut through to further clarify." He looked closer at the cuts on her arms. "It appears to be scratched from a tree or spiny bush of some kind. Will have to look at my assistant's notes and see if any debris was taken from these cuts."

He jotted another note and then removed the rest of the sheet to expose the lower half of her body. Her legs from the knees down had similar cuts and bruises as the arms. However, there was a distinct "I" sliced into her left thigh. We all inched closer to get a better view.

"Perhaps the killer wanted to leave a message, but ran out of time?" Luke looked to the doctor for any other ideas.

"Perhaps, although seeing as how they took the time to position her so deliberately at the fountain, I would think they had plenty of time to finish the message," I added.

The doctor looked from Luke to me and nodded his head.

"We will have to see if there are any other marks or clues this murderer has graced us with. Constable Weston, would you be a chum and help me turn her on her side? Perhaps there's more on the back of her leg," he said.

They gently turned her on her right side to get a view of the back of her legs, but nothing was distinguishable besides the same cuts and bruises we found on the rest of her limbs.

"No such luck, I'm afraid," Dr. Cannish said.

They gently placed her down on her back again. He looked at the bottom of her feet and after seeing nothing of note, began to gather his tools to begin the internal exam. I looked over to Luke and saw him pale a little at the site of the sharp instruments being arranged. He looked at me and gave me a tight smile. The doctor started to slice the abdomen open with a scalpel, and I could see Luke swaying a bit at the sight of the separating skin. I moved toward him and took an arm. I felt him lean into me a bit, but he nodded his head in reassurance.

"Should we get a bit of fresh air, Constable Weston? I think you need a glass of water. Did you get any rest at all since yesterday?"

"Ah yes, Miss Sweeting. I got about 2 hours rest, but I like that suggestion of fresh air. Perhaps a moment or two and a bit of coffee will help revive my spirits."

I led him out the double door and to an outside chair. He sat down and gulped in air. I called for Nate and told him to fetch some water for Luke. He returned with a glass in hand, and Luke took it gratefully, leaning his head back as he drank. I heard an exasperated sound coming from the doctor in the exam room and headed back in.

"Well, missy, you'll be shocked to hear about my newest discovery, I assure you!" He had this light of excitement I couldn't quite get behind while the poor dead girl laid cut open before me.

"It seems this girl was with child! A real conundrum now, I'd say." He placed the tiny fetus in a metal bowl and weighed it. "I'm going to say four to five months."

My heart sank as the sadness swelled within me. What monster would ravage an innocent mother-to-be? The resolve to help put this beast away strengthened within me. I would not stop until the culprit received their due.

"It's a boy!" I blanched at the doctor's vulgar sense of humor. I guess in his line of work, nothing is sacred anymore.

17

Chapter 17- Gossip and Earl Grey

Scandal, such sweet scandal. Has tea time ever been so stimulating?

"Are you out of your mind? You chased him down an alley! You could have been killed!"

Luke was not taking the events from the previous day very well at all.

"Yes, well, I needed to know. Besides, he hardly seems like the type of gentleman to give me a mode of protection and then just go off to harm a girl and frame me for it. It seems quite counterproductive if you ask me. I think he is quite innocent, and I haven't told you the rest yet," I said.

Luke prevented himself from replying. His strained features clearly related he had more to say on the subject.

I divulged the trail of the brooch as best that I could recollect, which, not bragging, was every particular. When I got to the bit about my cousin, Luke eyed me suspiciously for a few moments, then interrupted.

"So Miss Sweeting, you're telling me your cousin had it in his pocket at the very same party that the violinist was last seen alive?"

"Yes, but it was taken from his jacket during the party. He had given it to the coat attendant," I said.

76

"I'm not saying Mr. Nethersby is guilty, but it seems pretty convenient that it just happened to go missing from his pocket the same night the girl was murdered."

"Well, Constable Weston, it seems to me that is exactly what you are saying. However, it matters not, because my cousin and I are to attend tea this very afternoon with Lady Thetford, who has a promising lead on the brooch disappearance. I think, perhaps, you might want to follow up on trying to find out who the father-to-be might have been?" I replied with a huff.

The tension was building to a boiling point as we tried to unravel this mystery. If we didn't take a moment, I am unsure what accusations would then fly.

"Miss Annabelle, I am sorry. I didn't mean to come across that way." He combed his hand through his hair in frustration. "Yes, I will follow up on the father angle. I think I will go interview her band members and see if they have any knowledge of him."

I took in the clear fatigue weighing him down.

"I think, perhaps, you need a few more hours of sleep, Luke. You won't do her justice if your senses aren't sharp."

His eyes darted to mine as his Christian name slipped from my lips. A warm smile spread across his.

"Yes, I suppose you're right, Belle." He tested out my name tentatively. "Let's plan to meet tomorrow for luncheon and discuss what our leads have led to?"

My heart skipped a beat, and I felt a little guilty finding so much pleasure amidst a murder investigation. But, like my dear cousin, Jaime, would say, "We must not let the shade of death darken the brilliance of life, my dear Belle. Not one ounce!"

Jaime and I arrived at the Thetford dwelling precisely at the appointed time, and at the perfect moment to witness a most disgruntled maid's departure. Her exasperated expressions, as the housekeeper threw her traveling bags down the entrance steps, were anything but cordial. The frazzled maid swore under her breath as she collected her belongings.

"Are you alright, miss?" I gently touched her shoulder as she started to pass us.

"Ah, yes, well, no. You see, they are accusing me of stealing. I have never stolen nothing in my life, miss! They have no proof either, they just threw me out on my a… I mean, well, my backside, miss. Now, I'll never find a job with that kind of reputation!" She started to wipe her eyes and nose on a dainty worn handkerchief.

"I am sorry to hear that. What is it that you were to have stolen, if you don't mind me asking?" Jaime interjected.

"Something to do with metal flowers, I think, it was quite unclear. I promise though, I have nothing. They went through my rooms and all my belongings, and still they threw me out."

"What's your name, miss?"

"Ah, excuse me. I'm Gwen Vannery. I've only been working here for three months, but I thought that Lord Thetford liked me. He showed me a lot of kindness; I guess I was mistaken, though."

"Jaime, perhaps she can help around our place for a bit while she gets her bearings?" I looked at my cousin with big doey eyes.

"Oh, Cousin Belle! You and your strays. Yes, fine. Miss Vannery, go to this address on Bread Street and show this card to the butler, Stewart. He will get you situated. We will give you a trial run in the kitchen, we've been needing a little help lately anyway."

Gwen's big blue eyes shone with awe. She took the card Jaime held out and thanked us before dashing towards town.

"The description she gave of the stolen item has a small resemblance to my brooch, wouldn't you say, cousin?"

"You're the sleuth, my dear. I am only here for the tea." He winked at me and took my arm to escort me into the Thetford manor. We followed the housekeeper to the west parlor where Lady Thetford waited with a delightful spread of confections and tea. As we took our seats, she began pouring the steamy brew.

"This Earl Grey is the very best, fresh from Duncan's downtown. I hope you enjoy it. I just can't indulge subpar tea. It really leaves the palette vexed." Lady Thetford offered us sugar and lemon, but I declined both. Tea was meant to be tasted for its base flavors. I guess I'd be considered a purist that way.

"Thank you, Lady Thetford. This tea is divine and your setting is exquisite. I am most appreciative of your hospitality," I said.

"I second that emotion dear lady, quite fine indeed," Jaime said. He nodded his head toward Lady Thetford and raised his cup in appreciation.

"Oh, you are too kind, and please call me Talia! I have longed for some fine company and here you finally are." Her smile was so bright that I thought it might actually hurt her face.

"Yes, well now, Lady Talia, you said you have some information on my dear cousin's missing brooch? I am quite indebted to you with any information you can give us," Jaime inquired.

"Yes, Mr. Nethersby, I was quite shocked that one of my staff would dishonor the household so, but good help is hard to find, or so they say. I actually dismissed the offending servant this very morning. The coat attendant saw her rifling through several coats during the later dances, and I have no reason to doubt my attendant, as he has been with the family for many years now, I can have him brought in if you like?"

I just couldn't see the bewildered maid from this morning doing what Lady Thetford claimed. Every instinct told me there was more to this than she said.

"If you don't mind, I would like to talk to your attendant. Possibly before we leave, I wouldn't want to disrupt this most enjoyable visit. ," I said.

For a moment, I saw a slight grimace on Talia's face before it was replaced with a warm smile.

"Of course, Miss Annabelle. It is no trouble at all, I assure you."

We continued talking about the party and all the wonderful new fashions coming from Paris. I didn't really contribute to that part of the conversation, as I was more geared towards creating my own styles. Jaime was very engaged and loved to incorporate outside influences into his work. Plus, everyone knew Paris had the best dyed feathers. The conversation persisted on this topic for a good hour. So lost in the discussion, we were startled by the chime of the parlor clock.

"Ah, time flies when good company is enjoyed, does it not?" Talia rang the servant's bell to have the tea service cleared away.

"It does, indeed. Thank you again for your most amiable invitation. Before we depart, may I take a moment to talk to your attendant?" I watched Talia closely at my inquiry.

This time, she seemed even more discontented by my request. She recovered quickly and said she would call for the servant promptly. I thought it strange that she would offer us the chance to interview him if she was so inconvenienced by it.

"Callen, this is Miss Annabelle Sweeting and Mr. Jaime Nethersby. I want you to tell them what you told me regarding the party and the servant rifling through the coats." She raised her eyebrow as if to deter any objection to her request.

"Ah, yes mum, well like you said I was the coat attendant that evening. I saw the maid, Gwen, going through the coat racks looking for something when I came back from using the privy. I also saw a few couples sneaking some alone time behind the racks, and, of course, Lord Thetford was there for a bit, checking that the mechanics of the racks were keeping up."

"Ah yes, that will be all, Callen. You see, Miss Sweeting? We searched Gwen's things, but I fear she has already pawned it off, my dear," she said.

"Yes, I see. Um, Callen, would you be so kind as to show me the powder room?" I quickly jumped up and headed towards the door through which the attendant was leaving.

"Oh, it seems my cousin has rather enjoyed too much tea, Miss Talia." I heard Jaime's nervous laughter as I followed Callen out.

"Right this way, miss."

As we neared the room, I stopped him and pulled him aside.

"Callen, can you answer a question for me, please?"

"I'll do my best, miss."

"Yes, well, can you tell me… was Gwen alone when she was looking through the racks, or were the couples or Lord Thetford in there with her?"

"Ah, yes, the couples I was told not to tell you who they were for discretion's sake. But, um, they were not with Gwen when she was there."

"What about Lord Thetford?"

"Well, yes, he was, miss. I hate to say. The Lady would have my head for saying so, but I did see Lord Thetford leaving right before I went back in the room. That's when I saw Gwen still in there looking about."

"Did you see her looking in the pockets of the coats?"

"Ah, no. She was looking at the ground around the racks. I didn't actually see her look in a jacket, though."

"Thank you, Callen. You have been most helpful."

"You're welcome, miss." The last word was extended like the hiss of a snake.

He turned and headed to continue his duties. I went to the powder room and gathered my wits before returning to the parlor room to say our goodbyes. Talia seemed to be agitated when I returned. She inquired if Callen was able to shed any new information on the missing brooch. I told her he was very helpful but feared my bauble had been pawned already. I felt the need to omit information again, and she looked appeased by my response. Something nagged at my mind as I tried to put the pieces together. I needed to talk to Gwen Vannery again and soon.

18

Chapter 18- A New Beginning

Forgiveness is not a weakness. It is surely growth. At least that's what I'm telling myself.

Jaime and I headed out the front entrance towards Nathan and Purgy. Nate was conversing with Miro on the bottom of the stairs, and I instantly remembered my promise to allow him to accompany me home after tea. I felt horrible about the lapse in memory. It was quite unlike me, but I can only attribute it to the investigation taking up all my attention.

"Mr. Nassar, kind of you to meet us. I must admit I had quite forgotten our agreement to travel together, and as you can see, your sister-in-law requested my dear cousin to accompany me to tea this afternoon. I am afraid I do not require a ride home after all," I said.

His face was crestfallen as I delivered the news. I had not planned to go home anyway. I wanted to bring the goggles to Charles with my cousin, but before I could relay these intentions to Jaime, he said, "Oh cousin, nonsense. You need not have me mucking up your plans. I will head home and see how our new stray, I mean maid, is settling in. Besides, the conversation we had with Lady Thetford has me quite inspired to get some work in as well."

"If that is your desire, cousin? We can deliver the goggles tomorrow morning then, I suppose. Mr. Nassar was only going to escort me home, to begin with."

"Well, Miss Sweeting, since you are no longer needed by your cousin, then let us make an afternoon of it. I was hoping to show you some of the new items I was working on in my lab anyway, if you're interested?"

He knew he had me. The thought of seeing the newest gizmos and gadgets being developed was something I could not turn down.

"Mr. Nassar, I would be delighted to see your new prototypes."

"See cousin, what a wonderful idea. Have fun now, and try not to break anything," Jaime said as he took his leave.

Nathan hovered about, looking nervous and agitated.

"Nate, are you quite well?"

"Ah yes, miss, it's just that, I thought we'd be heading home is all, and so I had plans to have some laughs with some of the motor port boys."

"Nathan, you can go ahead and meet your friends. I have Purgy, and Mr. Nassar swears to be a gentleman as he accompanies me, so you don't need to feel any guilt about it, understood?"

He looked to Miro for confirmation, and Miro crossed his heart with his finger and smiled. Nate's face lit up with a smile, and he nodded. He tipped his hat and turned to run to catch a ride with Jaime. Purgatorio roared at his retreating back in goodbye.

"Well, it seems this beastie has taken a shine to both of you. That is interesting, as it was only meant to attach itself to one person. One main companion," Miro thought out loud.

"Let us be off, and I will show you some more creations that are quite astounding." He smiled as he escorted me to his motor. His peridot eyes reflected the sun just so, to make them sparkle with some hidden mirth he seemed to always possess. I smiled back shyly, not knowing why.

On the way to Miro's lab, Purgatorio shut down to recharge in the back seat. The whirling of his gears and the sounds of the city were like an industrial song filling me with possibilities. I closed my eyes to enjoy the sensation and a similar memory popped into my head of a pair of green eyes in a side mirror. I opened my eyes and turned towards Miro to see him staring at me once again, an expression of intense curiosity written on his face.

"What is it?"

"Ah, Miss Annabelle, I was just wondering where your mind goes. You have the most pleasant look on your face when you drift, and I wish I knew how to make it happen more often," he said.

My face heated up from the compliment, and I struggled to find a response.

"Say you forgive me for my omission of the optic lens. I most desperately beg your pardon. I would never intentionally inflict any kind of harm on you, Miss Sweeting. I was so overzealous in my need to test the mechanics that I quite lost my rational sense. I will not allow it to happen. I could not take it to see you unhappy with me again."

His declaration pulled at my heart, and I felt his sincerity.

"I forgive you, Mr. Nassar. Please, let us begin anew," I said.

"Oh no, I have to start all the way over?" He looked at me with sad puppy eyes. "I am now just a mere acquaintance you'll acknowledge with a slight head bow across the room. My poor heart can't take it," he replied.

I laughed at his dramatic proclamation.

"You know very well we are friends, Mr. Nassar. You do have such a flare for drama!"

"Well, since we are friends, Miss Annabelle, I give you permission to call me Miro. Now you must realize you are only of a select few that have this privilege and should feel quite special."

"I can well imagine," I said. The injured face he presented had me laughing all over again.

We pulled into the parking area for his building and I said, "Well, Miro, let's see what kind of diabolical contraptions you and your brother have in the works."

Miro smiled a satisfied grin and moved to exit the motor and get my door for me. Before he made it, the whirl from the back seat stopped, and Purgatorio pounced between the seats, ready for action. I scratched his chin plates, and he chuffed in appreciation. Miro opened my door, and Purgy and I exited together.

"The bigger building over there is my brother's section. He has many people under his watch creating fascinating devices. I am afraid we are not allowed to visit that section. He has a few government contracts that are quite hush-hush. However, I know he is working on a steam water purification system. I don't know the specifics, but it is said to be able to filter toxic particles out with heat. I think he is hoping to help the Brass Boroughs with their water supply. Over here is my building. I am not so geared towards philanthropy as my brother, but I do hope my creations will give some pleasure to the world," he explained.

I followed him into the front entry and down a long white hall. Several doors were on either side, but we did not slow our pace until we reached the last door on the left. He turned to me with a big grin before swinging the door open to reveal a large hangar-like area.

Within the space was a miniature airship. It was not a commercial liner like was common. It was a private airship for at most 4 people, and it was gorgeous. A deep red balloon with a gold swirling design led to a light wooden deck. The captain's hutch was encased with dark wood, brass framing, and beautiful hanging lanterns. The airship took up the center of the room and was the obvious show stopper, but as I let my eyes drift around the perimeter of the room, I saw more stations, tables had half-built mythical creatures like Purgy on them. Other stations had different sized telescopes with odd swivels and gears and even smaller airships with claws affixed to their bottoms. The last table had, what appeared to be, artificial mechanical arms.

It was hard to take in all the different and eye-catching creations. Miro was enjoying my awe-inspired silence as I moved about the space. We did a small tour around the room, and he gave me an overview of what he was hoping to accomplish.

"Come now, Miss Annabelle, I must have you see this creation. What do you think?"

He took me over to where the miniature airships with the claws hung and hovered. These airships had wings on top as well, quite peculiar. He had a few different sizes, and I tried to suss out what they could be for.

He took pleasure from watching me struggle through ideas. His ego was clearly enjoying stumping me. At the very last moment before conceding defeat, however, I turned to him and said, "Are they parcel carriers? The claws would hold the parcels and the ships would fly them around the city. I'm right, aren't I?"

He first reacted with surprise, then defeat, then utter exuberance that I pieced it out.

"Yes, are they not marvelous? What time could people save from going out and about if they could have these handy gizmos grab their parcels for them? Umm, they are only in the early planning stages, but I think it has merit. Do you?"

I was surprised that he would care for my opinion on the subject.

"Yes, I think it has serious merit. Not only for convenience, but in the scenario of, let's say, sickness," I replied.

"What do you mean?"

"I mean, for example, an area is hit with a terrible plague or illness, and putting more people in the area other than the required doctors and physicians would put them in peril. These devices can deliver food, medicine, and communications without endangering the outside population. There are really many possibilities, I'd say!"

"Oh, I had never even thought of that usage. Yes, I suppose I could be in the philanthropy business after all. Take that, Earl of Thetford!"

He twirled me around, and I laughed at his merriment. He brushed a stray strand of hair from my cheek and smiled.

"Next time, I will take you up in the airship. If you are nice, I might let you steer it," he said.

Somehow, the distance between us had shrunk. I could feel the warmth of his breath tickle my cheek, then the heat was replaced with a soft kiss. I looked up into his eyes as he took a step back.

"Now, we should get you home," he said.

Miro sounded like he wanted to do anything other than that. I shivered with the sudden loss of proximity. I felt it return as he took my arm and placed it in his. Miro led me out to the white hall, and we walked towards the exit. I felt something change between us. Perhaps, we were not friends after all?

19

Chapter 19- Another Murder

A tinker, a tasket, a gear, and a cog gasket. Another lovely day in London!

I felt like I was floating when I returned home. I barely acknowledged Stewart as I passed him in the entrance hall and made my way up to my room to change for dinner. I brushed my hair out in the looking glass and pressed my finger pads against the spot where he kissed me. It seemed strange to me to find my senses scrambled by such a small action. Clearly, I was unprepared for such overwhelming feelings, but I also felt a trace of guilt.

I sat down to dinner with Jaime and we discussed our plans for the morning.

"Oh, so we are to drop off the goggles at the blacksmith's then?" Jaime asked coyly.

"Yes, dear cousin, it's been an age, and I believe tomorrow is a discard day, as well. I wonder what marvelous metal bits we shall find."

"Oh, Belle, the things you find exciting are so strange sometimes, I swear! So, tell me more about this Charles fellow. Do you think he likes ices?"

"Jaime, he's a blacksmith who works near a hot furnace all day, I am sure he loves them," I laughed.

"Well, then perhaps I will ask him to have one while you are digging in the metal rubbish. I wonder if he's a plain lemon guy, or if he likes a more exotic fruit flavor?"

I looked wide-eyed at my cousin until he returned my gaze and laughed at my expression.

"Come now, Belle, do you know what Mr. Nassar's favorite ice is yet?"

I blushed at the question.

"Or perhaps, it's Constable Weston that has your preference?"

The guilt from earlier panged again, and I realized now where it originated. I was harboring feelings for both these gentlemen. How could I not see it until now? I have really been quite blind the last couple of days for a lady who prides herself on being so perceptive.

"Ah, I see you are realizing something just now, cousin. What will you do I wonder? Both choices are quite scrumptious if I do add my two pence. Mr. Nassar is full of exotic mystery, and he likes to tinker with mechanical contraptions as much as you do. But oh, a man in uniform. Ding, dong! Constable Weston is so dashing, and brave, and tends to match outfits with you."

"Cousin, I hadn't realized how fond of both of them I've grown, how could this happen? I am supposed to be exploring the city and experiencing the wonders of the industrial world with all its possibilities. Perhaps I should open my own shop or sell some of my creations at a local stand. That'd be better than being knee-deep in a murder investigation and a love triangle!"

"Love, already Belle? You do work fast, my dear."

"You know what I mean, Jaime! I wasn't expecting any of this."

"Well, that's the best part, isn't it? The unexpected. The dashing young constable, the rebellious younger son of an earl. By God, Belle, I think you're living my fantasy!"

As we stared at each other for several silent moments, a bubble of laughter started to surface, and before we knew it we were beyond hysterical. I could barely catch a breath as my eyes watered from the exertion. Jaime was still bent over breathing deeply when the maid came in with dessert. She quickly left when she saw the state we were in, and that had us giggling all over again.

"Oh Belle, have I told you how glad I am that you are staying with me? It truly is a blessing to have someone to laugh with. I didn't realize how much I'd missed it." He wiped his eyes and smiled at me.

"Jaime, it is I who am indebted to you for your kindness in letting me stay here," I said.

We finished our dessert in comfortable silence and prepared for an after-meal tea in the parlor room. A sudden thought hit me when the maid came in to take the plates, and I looked at Jaime in question.

"Cousin, where is the new maid, Miss Vannery? I haven't seen her all night. Is she doing well in the kitchen?"

"Oh, yes I inquired about her when I came home, and Stewart said she never showed. I thought it peculiar since she seemed so excited at the prospect," he said.

"That is quite odd."

After tea, I headed to bed and told Purgy to wind down at night so he wouldn't lose a chunk of time in the afternoon. He shook his mane from side to side in refusal. He sat on the floor at the foot of my bed like a silent sentry. I closed my eyes and drifted off. I dreamed of a dance where I was turning about constantly, and my partner's eyes continually changed from green to brown and back again.

I found Nathan ready and waiting for me as I entered the breakfast room the next day. He seemed unusually chipper for the early hour, and I wondered what he and his friends had gotten up to yesterday.

"Nathan, how are your motor port friends? And why are you so chipper this morning?"

"Ah, well missus, it's just, not exactly… proper talk, you see? You know what? I'll tell ya anyway, though, seeing as you're so interested. I won, I did! They were racing their motors around the tracks yesterday afternoon, and I bet a small amount on the underdog, cause he's my friend and all, and then what happens? He beats the lot of them! Can you imagine? I made two pounds, I did!"

"Well, I can't condone gambling. However, I must say those are quite the winnings! Congratulations!"

His smile beamed with my praise and he helped himself to a serving of eggs and bacon. I made my way through the station to fill my plate, and we sat and chatted while we ate. Purgatorio flew about the ceiling and swooped up and down enjoying the maids scrambling as he neared.

"Make sure to grab the rucksack today, Nate. We are going to the blacksmith's this morning and it's excess metal day! Let's go see where my cousin is and head out," I said.

"Yes, missus! But before we head out, I wanted to give you somethin'," he said shyly.

"It's just a token of thank you for bringing me along and hirin' me and all."

He pulled out an object wrapped in a pale blue cloth and handed the bundle to me. I unwrapped it carefully to reveal a beautiful hairpin wire wrapped in shiny copper and dark bronze tones. They encased a small beautiful piece of amethyst. My mouth dropped open in a very unladylike manner, and I quickly shut it.

"Nathan Starling! You shouldn't have spent so much on me. This is by far too generous."

He smiled with a mixture of relief and happiness.

"I'm glad you like it, missus. To be honest, I only bought the stone for a right fine bargain in the Boroughs. The rest I made with some of the scrap metal pieces we've collected," he said.

"Well it's gorgeous, Mr. Starling, and you are so talented! I might have to have you join me in my tinker room soon." I removed the hat I had on right then and there and quickly swapped the pin in its place. "How does it look?"

I tilted my head this way and that to model it for him. He smiled with pride and said, "It looks great, missus, just great!"

Jaime came rushing through the door, "Are you three coming or what?"

Clearly, he was too anxious to leave rather than break his fast.

"You must calm yourself, cousin, we're just finishing up. Take some scones for the road, you don't want your stomach grumbling at an inopportune time," I teased.

"Yes, quite right." He dashed to the breakfast bar and grabbed a few before turning and leading us out towards the door.

"By the way cousin, smashing new hairpin!"

"Why thank you, Jaime. Nathan made it for me," I replied.

"Did he, indeed? Quite striking, young sir."

I don't think Nate's chest could have gotten any more puffed out without popping a button on his vest. We headed out the door and toward my cousin's waiting motor. The trip to the smithy was quite jovial, and I took those moments to shine up the goggles one last time. We parked close to the alley where the scrap would be dispersed so I wouldn't have to walk too far to load it up for the ride home.

We were a bit early, but I knew Charles lived above his forge, so he would notice us soon enough. I stepped out and stretched my limbs. Jaime and Nathan headed towards the door, and I gave Jaime the goggles to present to Charles. He smiled and winked at me before turning towards the entrance. I walked around the back of the motor and grabbed my rucksack from the boot. I could hear Purgy's talons clicking behind me as I went.

Charles opened the door with a smile and told us to move toward the big garage door as he was about to open it up. He looked at me and shouted that he had already discarded a load of scraps in the back alley last night if I wanted to look. He laughed as I jumped up and down in excitement.

I turned from the others and headed into the darkened alley. It hadn't quite received the dawn's light yet. I saw a pale white object hanging above the pile of discarded metal. It was on a steel ladder that led to the roof. I squinted my eyes as I walked closer, unclear on what I was looking at.

Purgatorio hissed from behind me, and I felt the hairs on my neck stand up as the form took shape. I started running towards it, and I gasped as the recognition of her features penetrated my mind. The pale face of the maid, Gwen Vannery, was frozen in a scream towards the sky. Her limbs flared out from her like a ballerina reaching towards her beau. Purgatorio roared.

20

Chapter 20- The Dark Swan

The heart of a shadow is a mystery; bring the mystery to light, and there is nothing to fear, or is there?

I didn't scream, wail, or fall to my knees like a helpless damsel. I stood stoic, thinking, and completely confused by the posed body above me. Another dead woman bared before me in a scene as beautiful as it was brutal. These women were arranged as if they were morbid dancers placed on gruesome stages. I had the growing fear that they were placed specifically in *my* path. It just seemed too coincidental.

Sure, the first time it was in a park where anyone might happen to take strolls, but this one. This one tore at my senses. Who knew that I was to be at the blacksmith's today? Who was targeting these women? Who was making sure I saw them? Was this a warning? Before any of these questions could be answered, I needed to get Luke here straight away.

"Purgatorio, go get Nathan and Jaime and show them where I am, after that please go to the Yard and signal Constable Weston. Do you think you can do that for me?"

He chuffed in response. Purgy eyed the alley and made sure no one else was there before taking flight and heading to the forge where the others were. I returned my gaze upward to the scene and watched drops of blood continue to pool below Miss Vannery. I looked for any clues or a weapon that might have been used.

It was clear her throat was slashed in the same manner as the violinist. Her hands, clasped tight, no doubt hiding another couple of taunting tokens from the killer. Gwen's body had been tied up with leather bindings along the ladder, and long pieces of metal tied to her arms kept her pose in place.

Jaime, Charles, and Nathan were soon running down the alley.

"Belle, are you alright? What in God's name is going on? We must get the constable at once!"

"Calm yourself, cousin. Yes, I am fine. I sent Purgy to retrieve the constable, and I am hoping to figure out just what is going on," I said.

"Miss Sweeting, I assure you there was nothing like this in the alley last night. I….I don't know how…."

Charles started to sway as he looked up at the body. Jaime swooped in and held him upright as the strong man paled to the same shade as the body above us.

"Mr. Kaplan, I am quite certain you had nothing to do with this. Did you hear anything last night?"

"Well, I…. I put the metal scraps out around 11:30, and then I went to the pub down the way for a couple hours to unwind. I got back around two in the morning. I fell asleep right after, and I didn't hear a thing. Oh, look at her, her….throat. It's so… bloody." He looked like he was about to lose his breakfast.

"Jaime, take Mr. Kaplan to get some ices. I think he needs to get some fresh air and they might soothe his stomach. Nathan, you'll stay here with me while we wait for the constable, yes?"

I didn't know where this new assertive version of myself came from, but I liked it.

"Belle, are you sure you don't need me to stay? I don't want to leave you with this ghastly scene," Jaime said.

"I assure you, sir, I won't let anyone hurt her. I've got me pocket knife with me and will block her from any harm!" Nathan addressed Jaime with such passion, I was very moved by his protectiveness. Nathan showed the sharp dagger to Jaime, and Charles started swaying all over again.

"Yes, okay, young Starling. You take good care of my cousin. I will take Mr. Kaplan to Evanston's down the street. Please send word when the constable gets here so I am not biting my nails in worry," he said.

I nodded in affirmation, and the two set out back down the alley. Charles looked stronger the farther away he got from the body. I couldn't imagine such a strong man being so violently affected by the death. I guess that is why they call them gentle giants.

I could hear the muffled engine of my cousin's motor as they started up and drove away from the curb. My cousin got to go for ices after all. I shook my head at my wandering thoughts. I needed to be here, in this alley, with Gwen and figure out how this horrible thing happened.

"Nate, can you check for anything strange behind the bins over there? I will look in the metal debris and see if anything was dropped." I had several extra buttons in my rucksack that I handed to him to mark anything of interest. "We are looking for footprints in the dirt, bloody objects, anything you think is out of place for this alley, ok?"

"Yes, missus. On it!"

I heard several rumbling motors coming down the road before their shadows passed the alley mouth. Purgatorio swooped from the sky and roared to signal my location. A squeal of tires sounded as the motors parked, and at the head of the group, Luke appeared. He made brief eye contact with me before turning to his men.

"Block it off boys! Simon, we'll need the toolbox. Doctor Cannish, bring the gurney. Georgie, take some lads and see if any of the neighbors heard anything!"

He strode towards me with a warring expression of concern and relief. I wasn't expecting it, but he gathered me in his arms and hugged me tight against his chest.

"I almost lost my mind when I saw that beastie coming up to me without you. It was screeching to high heaven. I was able to suss out that you were okay. I don't know what I would have done if it were you, Belle." He released me a bit so he could look into my eyes. "Please don't scare me like that again, " he whispered.

"I'm sorry, Luke. I just came upon the scene and thought of the fastest way to get you here. I'm okay, but to be honest, I'm a bit frightened. It seems like these murders are being put directly in my path. Like a warning, or a threat, maybe?"

He hugged me tightly again and gently stroked my hair. I leaned into him, more this time, savoring the security I felt there. He released me fully when a throat cleared behind us.

"Well, I see we have another one, Miss Sweeting. Seems you have a knack for attracting the dead. I thought that was my specialty," said Dr. Cannish. "Now Constable Weston, do your duty so I can take this lady back to examine her. Chief Inspector Farthing is all a-tizzy about this new development. I, for one, do not want to be on his bad side, hey?"

"Yes, doctor. I will scan the scene quickly," Luke replied.

"Nathan and I put buttons near items of interest for you. Nathan found a boot print over there by the ladder, we tried not to disturb anything before you got here. I am pretty sure she has objects encased in her hands again, as well," I said.

He grimaced. "Yes, I am guessing you are correct. It took some doing and strength to get her up there. I do not believe this is the work of just one person, or if it is, they are finding the time to make it look seamless. We will catch them, though. I have a feeling something is about to break."

"Nathan, please go tell my cousin that the constable has arrived so he doesn't worry," I said. He tipped his hat to the constable and took off down towards the alley's mouth.

Luke canvassed the area and took note of all our buttons. He then examined the body from its perch and made several sketches in his notepad. He called forth a few officers to help cut her from her leather bindings and then proceeded to look for clues while she lay down.

Doctor Cannish offered him forceps to pry open the hands. He took the left one first. As he wedged the fingers open, they didn't seem as hard to open as Katherine's. I thought it was because Gwen hadn't been there as long. Inside her hand was a red stained calling card. The same one Jaime had given her the previous day. Luke looked at me, but I wasn't surprised. This killer was toying with me. I knew that for certain now.

Inside the right hand was another cryptic piece of paper. It contained part of an etching and the letter "A". He placed both items between the clean sheets of his notebook. Before he closed it, I leaned in and fanned my hand towards my nose over the calling card. He looked at me in question.

"It has the faint scent of petrol. Like it was in a garage, or a leaking motor hall," I said.

He did the same and nodded in agreement. Luke had his men gather a few more items, and then they placed her on the awaiting gurney. Doctor Cannish covered and wheeled her out of the alley. I watched her small hidden form recede, and I couldn't help thinking it was all my fault.

21

Chapter 21- Cold As Ices

"Do not be afraid: our fate cannot be taken from us, it is a gift." - Dante Alighieri

Purgatorio shut down as soon as we entered Constable Weston's motor. Luke needed to interview Mr. Kaplan, so we went to Evanston's to regroup with Jaime. We rode in silence as our collective thoughts were on the possible next steps we would need to take to get this set of murders solved. I knew the random scraps of paper were important, but I couldn't make out the image yet. Another thought popped into my head.

"Do you think she has something cut into her leg too?"

Luke looked at me in surprise. I had startled him from his own thoughts.

"Yes, that could be a possibility. We will have to follow up with Doctor Cannish after his examination," he said. "Belle, I really do not like how this killer seems to be focusing on you. I don't think you should be alone for even one moment. I know you have the beastie and Starling watching your back, let's keep it that way, okay?"

"Of course, Luke. I have enough common sense, especially after this

100

morning, to see the pattern that is emerging. I, by no means, want to give them the opportunity to get to me," I said.

He took my hand in his, and I felt a buzz fill my skin at the contact. We sat outside of Evanston's for a few more moments, then I woke up Purgy, and we made our way inside.

Luke guided me towards the door and opened it for us. I looked up and gave him a brave smile, although I felt anything but. We found Jaime and Charles at a table near the back. Nathan talked to them animatedly, and Charles looked a bit green around the gills as he listened. No doubt Nate was telling him more details about the gruesome scene we had just left.

"Cousin! You are here, finally. I am glad to see you too, Constable Weston, although not in such circumstances, I assure you," Jaime said.

"Yes, cousin, it has been quite a morning. Miss Vannery has been taken in for an examination, and Constable Weston and I still need to discuss our findings from yesterday. I thought we would join you here, rather than sit in the morgue."

"Yes, yes do. We need to stay close to you now, I think. Don't you, constable?"

"Yes, Mr. Nethersby. I was just telling Miss Sweeting that very thing on the way over here. She is not to be alone for one moment, as I do not like where these clues are leading. Unfortunately, I must ask you and Mr. Kaplan a few questions now," replied Luke.

To lighten the mood, Luke handed me some money for ices and said, "My treat."

I smiled and asked him what flavor he wanted. I headed up to the cashier to order for Luke, Nate, and me. I took my time at the counter and watched as Luke showed my cousin the card in his notebook. I saw Jaime gasp audibly and place his hand on his chest. Fevered whispers then ensued. I can only guess my cousin proclaimed his innocence while Mr. Kaplan patted his shoulder in support.

I found myself scanning the room. Nate was perched on a wall just behind Constable Weston, taking in all that was said. He glanced at me and tipped his hat. I pointed to my ear and then back at him, and he nodded. I continued my scan of the room and saw a few patrons I didn't know. However, Miss Whitney Cosswald and her maid sat near the window in the front corner. It wasn't so much that she was there for ices, but the fact that she wasn't with her sister, was quite striking. Her face was slightly covered by a lace screen hanging from her hat. I wondered why she took the time, as the outlandish outfit gave her away.

When I finished overlooking the store, I found Purgatorio staring back at me from just inside the front door. He pawed the floor and pointed his scorpion tail towards the right. He was directing me towards something outside. I nodded towards him and scooped up the ices to return to the table first.

"Here we are, gents. I am just going to say hello to Miss Cosswald over there, won't be a moment," I said.

They nodded and didn't pay me much mind as they continued their dissection of what occurred the night before. I signaled to Nate to follow me. I wasn't about to be caught blind-sided if anything was amiss.

I went towards Purgy and out the door towards the right. Nate followed not too close but like a stealthy little shadow. I saw a figure standing down the lane by the back entrance to Evanston's, and I edged closer to their position. It was One-eyed Whitmore, and he looked terrible. His nose was swollen, and his cheek bruised. When Nate recognized him, he rushed to my side. Whitmore beckoned us to come closer to him.

"What has happened to you, sir?"

"Oh miss, it's been terrible, it has! That bloody demon in the shadows won't let me be with them bloody tinkling bells. Fairies from hell, I swear it, but enough of that, miss. You need to know. There's talk in the Boroughs about ya, there is. They're saying you'll be next! I knew you were going to be faced with danger, but naught like this, my dear. Please be careful and watch your back! Whoever is chasing me thinks I knows him. But I don't, I swear it. At least, I don't think I do," he said.

"One-eye, where ya hearing the talk about the missus? Was it down by the docks, or by the Shady Calf? We need to know where ye are gettin' the story, we do," Nate said. His Brass accent came out as his anxiety grew.

"Ah yes, Starling, swooping in like a right bird, you are. It was at Tappers, you know the place? It's where the uppers' servants run off to when they can."

Nathan nodded.

"Servants, did you say?"

"Yes, miss. They don't want to be caught havin' a good time from their employers, you see? So they must spirit away to the Boroughs to have some fun, '' Whitmore said.

"Nathan, can you, very carefully, go to this pub and see if any servants we know frequent the place? I have a rather large suspicion that we are going to find a connection there," I said.

"Yes, missus. I know a couple of Brasses there, they do right by me. I will check it out tonight and hears what they have to say."

I turned at the sound of metal tapping the pavement. Purgatorio was signaling us that someone was coming.

"Whitmore, are you sure you don't want to go to the Bobbies with this? They could protect you if you told them what you know."

"No my dear, I won't. They have it in for me, they do. A scapegoat to pin it all on, I am sure of it. No, I'll take my chances out here. I just needed to tell ya."

I gave him a few shillings and told him to hurry up, as I was certain Luke was just around the corner. Whitmore ran down the side lane and disappeared among the crowds perusing the outside wares.

Luke stood at the corner of the lane next to Purgatorio. He clearly had seen One-eyed Whitmore run away and looked accusingly at me. Nathan and I walked back towards him and said nothing. His expectant eyes followed me as I returned to Evanston's.

"Your ices were melting, Miss Sweeting. Miss Cosswald sure looks worse for wear, I'd say. Anything interesting she had to tell you?"

"As a matter of fact, there was a lead I intend to follow. If you are done with your interviews, we can sit down and go over all we've learned in the last day or two."

We headed to our table in the back. I noticed Miss Cosswald was now joined by Lady Thetford and went to say a quick hello. They were deep in whispers when I approached and stopped abruptly at my closeness.

"Lady Thetford. Miss Cosswald."

I curtsied in greeting.

"It is so nice to see you both this morning. A ray of sunshine on a stormy start," I said.

"Ah, Miss Sweeting, you are looking quite well for what I hear has been a very trying morning, indeed! Oh, horrible, and I heard it was my poor servant. Perhaps I was too hasty in relieving her? Oh, it is all so vexing."

Miss Cosswald patted her hand, and Talia looked up at me from behind her lashes. She appeared small as if I were sent to chastise her for stealing a biscuit.

"Miss Sweeting, who do you think can be doing such horrific things? I hope this doesn't force people to cancel their events. I was so looking forward to the dance at the Bergenhalt's. I just received my invite this morning! I am sure, after your splash at the Thetford's, you will be invited as well," Whitney prattled.

"I know not, Miss Cosswald, but I hope to find out very soon," I replied.

Lady Thetford shuddered, and Miss Cosswald continued to pat her hand in comfort.

"Miss Whitney, I am surprised to not see your sister here. Is she alright?"

"Why yes, she is fine. Cara did have quite a headache this morning. I know it must be quite queer to see us apart. However, it is refreshing to get a word in," she said.

We all giggled at that and then sighed.

"Well, I will not detain you further from your visit; try and have a splendid day. I would say we should look forward to that dance, Miss Cosswald. I think if nothing else, it will keep our minds engaged instead of worrying about the latest ghastly events," I said.

I curtsied to them both again and took my leave. As I walked towards the table where Luke and Nate sat, I heard a jingling behind me. It was Lady Thetford's servant, Callen, bringing a fan to her. His walking boots had loose buckles that jingled when he walked. He ducked his head and grimaced at my notice. I was jostled out of my thoughts as I collided into a wall of chest.

"Pardon me, sir, I was looking behind me instead of in front as I should have," I said.

"Oh cousin, it's just me! I am going to take Mr. Kaplan back to his forge, and finally give him your goggles. I know you have much to talk to Constable Weston about. Do you want me to wait to give him the goggles?"

"Oh Jaime, yes that would be fine if you want to give them to him. Let me know how he likes them, and please take the rucksack from your boot and fill up anything that looks interesting from the stuff he didn't dispose of last night," I replied.

"Yes, Belle, I will take on this task for you," he said with an air of a knight going on a quest. "Dinner tonight, pray?"

"I am not sure. I do not know how long I will be going over what we have. I do not wish you to wait on my behalf. Let us have lunch on the morrow?"

"I am to have luncheon with Lady Whipley and Lord Thetford. I meant to ask you about attending last night, but I forgot. Oh my nerves, dear cousin. Well, that works out fine then, doesn't it? Please let Stewart notify me when you return tonight, I fear I won't rest easy until I know you are safe at home," he said.

I kissed his cheek and watched them leave. I also noticed that both Miss Cosswald and Lady Thetford had left. I walked back to the table where Luke sat waiting with his notebook open. I took out my own notebook that I had started carrying and sat across from him.

We stared at each other for a few moments and then he said, "Ladies first."

$$22$$

Chapter 22- Digging Deeper

We had barely scratched the surface, but I knew we'd find something rotten inside.

We had been there for hours, pouring over the notes we had collected. Each clue was more confusing than the last. Each conversation was suspect. I didn't know how we would sift through all the nonsense to get to the truth. My stomach growled, and I looked up at Luke in embarrassment.

"Oh, Miss Sweeting, I apologize. Of course, you are hungry. Let us go get some of those delicious meat pies your cousin told me you are fond of at Claymore's?"

"You've been discussing me with my cousin, have you? How interesting. And what all was discussed, sir?"

"Oh, just this and that really," he replied coyly.

"Perhaps I shall discuss this and that with your aunt tomorrow at luncheon," I said.

He raised his eyebrow at me and smirked. I chuckled at his expression and gathered my things to head to Claymore's. Nate headed out earlier to scope out Tappers and meet with his Brass contacts in the Boroughs.

Purgatorio fluttered to life as we neared the front entrance. We opened the door, and Miro exited his motor and headed towards us. He raked his hands through his hair as he walked, looking down. He lifted his head and widened his eyes as he noticed me in front of him.

"Annabelle, I just found out from Talia that you were here. I heard about the dreadful events of this morning and rushed over. I was in my lab all morning, so I hadn't learned of it until now. Are you okay?"

He grabbed my shoulders and looked me up and down to confirm I was in one piece.

"Mr. Nassar, thank you for your concern. As you can see I am fine, but a bit tired. Constable Weston and I were headed to Claymore's to get a bite to eat, do you wish to join us?"

Mr. Nassar finally noticed Luke standing beside me and greeted him gruffly. Luke returned his greeting with a slightly more civil hello.

"Ah no, I can see you are busy with your investigation, Miss Sweeting. I think you are to take lunch tomorrow with my brother, yes?" I nodded. "Yes, well then I will see you tomorrow." He rushed off towards his motor before I could say more.

"It seems you have quite a few people out of sorts, Belle. Did you still want to eat or did you want me to take you home to "rest up" for your lunch tomorrow?"

"Luke, don't act so wounded. Let's go to Claymore's and eat before you throw a tantrum. Besides, I have a few more details I need to sort out before we call it a night," I replied.

He looked defiantly at me but opened the passenger door for me. I climbed in, and Purgy flew to the back seat. Luke sat down and started the engine looking over at me. I peered back in question. He sighed and began to speak.

"Belle, I…. Well, I think you know I care for you, and I don't want to start anything just now, as we are in dangerous territory with this murderer on the loose. But I am hoping, when this investigation is concluded, that you might do me the honor of attending a dance or two with me?"

I could feel my face flush with color as he voiced his wishes out loud. He looked at me with a mixture of hope and trepidation as he waited for my response.

"Luke, initially I came to London to experience the industrial opportunities, and perhaps explore my own talents in a pursuit of selling my creations, or opening a shop. It would be an understatement to say my plans have been considerably derailed. "

His face took on a crestfallen expression. I quickly continued before he solidified the wrong impression I was apparently relaying.

"However, I have found myself growing attached to your friendship as well. I will not be dishonest and say I am not fond of Mr. Nassar. But also, in truth, I wish to get to know you better as well. I.... I think that I would be quite amenable to the idea of us going out in public together to dances to further our acquaintance. I cannot claim to be exclusively yours in the future until I know your true character," I finished.

His grin broadened as I fumbled through my declaration.

"So what you are saying is yes, but that I will have to fight for you with Mr. Nassar, hey? Well, aren't you a jewel to be had, Miss Sweeting."

I blanched at that and tried to say that it was nothing like that, but my words failed me.

"Oh, come now, Belle. Once this investigation is over, you best be prepared. I am going to charm you off your feet. Mr. Nassar doesn't stand a chance." He mouth curved into a devilishly rakish smile at this and took off down the street towards Claymore's.

All conversation about future courtship was left in the motor as we ate our meat pies and focused on the case. He had told me about the interview with Katherine's band members. Apparently, they did know she had a sweetie on the side, but they didn't know who. The piccolo player said he didn't think it was on the up and up. As in, the suitor was married or far above her station. He also said he saw Mr. Cosswald hanging about her the night of the dance. He peppered her with questions on the technique she was using. The band member found this quite amusing as Mr. Cosswald was by no means a musician. He just had a bell he liked to carry in his jacket pocket to get servants' attention.

I couldn't recall meeting Mr. Cosswald. I would have thought he would be apparent by way of dress like the rest of his family. Perhaps things were not as wonderful at home as the daughters seem to portray it. I added it to my list to follow up on.

I told him of One-eyed Whitmore's warning, of the tea we had with Lady Thetford, and what her servant Callen had told me. I could feel the pieces were there, but I couldn't fit them together yet. Something just wasn't connecting.

23

Chapter 23- Falling Flat

Remember that facing one's own failure is how we grow. Please let that be true!

Purgatorio and I returned home, and I staggered through the hall past Stewart on my way to my bed-chamber. I didn't even know what he was wearing; I couldn't concentrate. All the other ideas coursing through my brain were too demanding.

"Can you let my cousin know I made it home, Stewart?"

"Yes, milady. I'll have a maid bring up some tea, you could use some before bed, I think," he replied.

I think that was the kindest he has ever been to me. Perhaps my pitiable state was more apparent than I realized.

"Is Nathan home yet, sir?"

"Yes, he returned about a half-hour ago. Young Starling is down in the kitchen eating some leftover dinner. Should I send him up with your tea instead?"

"Yes, please. Thank you, Stewart. You have been most helpful."

He smiled, took my coat, and gently pushed me up the first few stairs. I opened my door and found my nightwear waiting for me on my bed.

It seemed someone had been anticipating my lateness. As I picked up the items and headed for the changing screen, a note fluttered to the ground.

Dear Belle,

Please do take care these next few days. The more I think about this investigation, the more I worry about you. Please don't think me too overbearing, but I can't imagine what I would do if something were to happen to you.

Your dearest cousin,

J.A. Nethersby

P.S. Your rucksack is in your makeshift studio. Charles put in a few extra pieces for you. He loved the goggles!

I held the note to my chest and heaved a heavy sigh. It seemed everyone was so concerned about me. The weight of their worry was more oppressive than my own fears. Clearly, I realized the danger of being so intimately entangled with this murder investigation, but I would have been even more scared if I was waiting on the sidelines. I could not bear to not contribute, sitting on my hands while this madman scurried around in the dark, plotting and killing.

These thoughts were not productive. Why should I worry about what I could not control? If I worked the puzzle and found the connections, then the murderer would never get to me. We would catch them. We had to.

My resolve strengthened, and I finished dressing for bed. I gently lay the beautiful hairpin and dagger bracer down on my vanity. A knock roused me from my thoughts, and Nathan came in with tea service and a plate of biscuits.

"Ow, missus, the butler told me you was a frightful mess, so I thoughts

I should bring you some treats too. Those always set me to rights," he said.

I laughed at that. "Yes, I suppose I did look like quite a scarecrow. It has been a harrowing day, for sure. Did you fare better in the Boroughs, Nate?"

"Oh, did I, missus! One-eye was right; all the uppers' servants hang about that place. I even saw Chelsey Smithers, your cousin's own kitchen maid, playing some sort of card game in the back. She was rambling on about the luncheon you are all to attend tomorrow. A right chatterbox, that one!"

"Oh, my. Who else did you see that we might know?"

"There was the Cosswalds' maid, the coat attendant chap from the Thetford mansion, the piccolo and percussion player from the band, and that assistant from the fabric shop we visited. That's all I remember seeing, but I did get distracted by a brawl," he said.

"A brawl? That seems like an unlikely place for one, with all the servants from well established families. Did you know the fighting parties?"

"One was the betting bookmaker at the motor garage races, and the other looked like a sore loser to me, missus. I couldn't tell you who he was, but if I saw him again, I'm sure to tell ya," he said.

I drank my tea and mulled over the things Nathan had told me. I couldn't think as clearly as I would like and decided to leave it for morning reflection. I bid Nathan a good evening and drifted off into a dreamless sleep. I knew any dreams would be nothing but nightmares.

I woke up later than usual, but that was expected after the previous day's adventures. I stretched and tried to release the tightness in my muscles. I was about to dress in my tinkering clothes but recalled at the last moment that I was to have a luncheon with Jaime and the Thetfords. To say I wasn't looking forward to it would be an understatement. All I wanted was to work on my mechanical creations, dwell within myself a bit, and let the last few days sift themselves out into some form of coherent picture. Perhaps the luncheon would not last too long, but I felt there would be little chance of that occurring.

I brushed out my hair and wound it into a bun. I fixed my amethyst hairpin and fastened my bracer on my right wrist. I wore my lavender corset with steel gray buttons and my red half skirt with buckskin breeches below. I had buckskin short gloves to match. I finished it off with my dark leather half jacket which buckled at the neck. I smiled in the mirror, but I could see that it didn't reach my eyes. When I was such a bad company even to myself, how could I bear several hours of polite society? Time would tell.

"Well, cousin, it took you long enough to come down. You missed breakfast completely, but I suppose that was to be expected after your evening out with the constable. I hope it wasn't all ghastly murder talk."

He looked at me expecting a reply. When I didn't respond, he said, "Well, I guess, when dealing with crimes, pleasantries may be left on the wayside, yes? Speaking of pleasantries, we've got an invite to the Bergenhalt's dance this weekend. I daresay we must attend. They are said to have quite the shindig. I, for one, am looking forward to the servants' garments. They are said to do a theme for each dance, and Lady Whipley told me that last year it was Hansel and Gretel. Could you imagine? The footman was a gingerbread man! Their confection table was something of legend," he squealed.

"Well, cousin, we must go then! I wonder what the theme will be this year? Have they said in the invitation?"

He smiled at my new found enthusiasm and interest.

"Oh, Belle, it is to be quite shocking, I assure you! This year it is to be the seven deadly sins!"

"I hope it will be done tastefully and without too much scandal. I daresay there are young ladies attending. The Miss Cosswalds, I understood, were planning to go. We shall have to see if Lady Whipley knows anything else about the details at luncheon," I said.

"Yes, dear cousin, she has been commissioned with the designs of the servants' attire. She has taken it all on herself and has kept it quite hidden from me. We will have to pry some details out of her this afternoon, indeed!"

24

Chapter 24- Social Butterfly

Is it just me, or do you find murder to be quite the conversation starter?

We arrived precisely at the appointed time at Lady Whipley's beautiful brick suites on Broad Street. Everything was ridiculously clean and properly positioned. I felt quite out of place. However, once we entered the dining hall, a different atmosphere took over.

Mouth-watering smells and cheerful laughter floated through the room like music. Lady Whipley came to greet us and took us each by hand. Her smile was contagious and welcoming. The starkness of her front rooms was driven away by the warmth and comfort of the dining hall.

"Thank you for coming to my little gathering. Mr. Nethersby, it is great to see you as always, and your divine cousin, Miss Sweeting. I've heard of your trying couple of weeks, my dear. I hope that any hardships can be forgotten at the door here, at least for a little while," she said.

"Lady Whipley, you are too kind. We were more than honored to receive your invitation, and I believe I can speak for my cousin. We would be glad to take any diversion you can supply at the moment,"

Jaime said. I nodded my head in agreement, and we were led to our seats.

Several guests were already there, including Lady Bergenhalt, Mr. and Mrs. Cosswald, and their daughters. I understood from my cousin that the last to arrive would be Lord and Lady Thetford and Miro, as he had indicated the previous day. Everyone was excitedly talking about what the Bergenhalt outfits might consist of this year. Lady Bergenhalt was laughing immensely as the ideas were more and more outlandish and provocative. She did not, however, yield any clues on the subject, to the great vexation of all.

Lord and Lady Thetford arrived approximately twenty minutes later and were bickering back and forth as they entered the dining hall. I only caught a few words, but there seemed to be some dispute about pantaloons. Miro trailed in, slightly after them, with an embarrassed smirk as he made his way to the last empty seat across from me. Mr. Callen, Lady Thetford's manservant, came in and whispered something in her ear.

"Yes, yes, fine. Be off with you. I need not hold your hand to do such simple tasks," she dismissed him harshly. His loose boot buckles chimed with urgency as he left the room.

Talia and Lord Thetford sat adjacent on the right side of the table to Lady Whipley, who sat at the head. Next to Lord Thetford was his brother Miro. The two Cosswald girls were on the end. Lady Bergenhalt sat opposite Lady Thetford, followed by Jaime, myself, and Mr. and Mrs. Cosswald. Miro smiled as he took his seat across from me and rolled his eyes at his brother and sister-in-law. I smiled back.

Before we could say anything, Lord Thetford said, "Well then, Miss Sweeting, how are you on this fine day? I can see that you are well, indeed. My brother has told me such terrible things about the last few days that you have had to face, and I must say you are holding up tolerably well for a young lady. I am sure Lady Talia would have fallen faint straight away, wouldn't you, my dear?"

Lady Talia's face turned quite sour at his declaration. "Oh, Oliver, you exaggerate. I am no wilting flower. I assure you. Perhaps if you spent a little more time at home instead of your lab, you would recognize that," she quipped.

"Sure, sure, darling. But I do recall you swooning last month to a spider in the hallway. Can you deny it?"

"Spiders are terrifying, sir! Much more hideous than any dead body, I assure you," she said.

That earned a chuckle from several listeners. The look on Lady Thetford's face said she did not think it was funny at all.

"Don't fret, my love. We could all take a note from Miss Sweeting's book. Such nerve and logic are rarely bestowed in such a pretty package," he said.

"I definitely second that," said Miro.

I blushed and turned to find Lady Thetford's narrowed eyes throwing imaginary daggers at me. She caught my returned glance and schooled her face back to a pleasant neutral. It was quite frightening to see her anger directed at me. I was jostled from my thoughts by an elbow from my left.

"Well, cousin, you sure seem to make an impression even when you sit there doing or saying nothing," he whispered conspiratorially. "Lord Thetford has shown you more notice than anybody, besides his machines, in quite some time."

"I can't imagine why. We had barely talked at the dance. He must have heard an account from Mr. Nassar," I whispered back.

"We know Mr. Nassar would sing your praises, now don't we?" He winked at me then continued. "I thought, however, that with their rivalry he would be a little less outspoken on the subject."

"You mean me? I'm the subject?"

He gave me a little smirk.

"But cousin, how can that matter when Lord Thetford is quite married? There would be no competition," I said.

"My dear, naive cousin. Not all marriages are like fairy tales. Sometimes, gentlemen are not very gentlemanly at all."

Stunned, I found my eyes dart towards Lord Thetford. He was staring at me with a sly smile, and I shivered.

Fortunately, all conversations around us had returned to the upcoming dance. There was talk on what dresses would be worn, what new fashions Lady Whipley had seen coming out of Paris recently, and the like. The soup was served, and conversation died down for a few moments while we enjoyed the apple parsnip concoction the kitchen had created. Served with rosemary herb bread, it was quite delicious.

Mr. Cosswald next to me had yet to speak two words together. That changed as he brought out his little servant's bell to ring for another bowl. He turned to me with glowing eyes and started trying to decode all the flavors and spices of the soup until his next bowl arrived. I've never seen a man so enthralled by soup, but I joined in as his excitement was contagious. He was thrilled when I mentioned the hint of ginger that he had not picked up on yet.

Mrs. Cosswald just shook her head good-humorously and continued her discussion with the girls on the embellishments they would have to add to their dresses for the dance. Their comfort with each other contradicted Luke's evidence from Katherine's band members that they did not get along. The Cosswalds clearly accepted each other's oddities and took them in stride. That bell of his was still quite jarring, though.

The next few courses went by without incident, and the kitchen produced some truly delicious dishes. The smoked pheasant was served with an orange sauce. Glazed green beans with almonds, fire-roasted chestnuts with ham and shallots, followed. Each dish was as rich with flavor as the last. I closed my eyes to enjoy a bite and opened them to find a pair of green ones watching me.

"Ah, Mr. Nassar. You've caught me again, I see. Do you not agree that this meal is quite exquisite?"

He smiled at me with a hint of amusement. "Yes, Miss Sweeting, I would say this is one of the best luncheons I have ever attended. The food is grand, but the company is just as desirable."

To cover the blush that I felt growing, I launched into a different subject.

"So, Nathan has told me of the motor races, and I remember you telling me that the cab you picked me up in was actually one such vehicle. Have you done any racing, sir?"

I heard a scoff from his left and watched his brother as he waited for Miro's answer.

"Oh, my motor has made great strides, as a matter of fact! We just added some new grit-resistant tires, slimmed down the roof for a more angled approach, and enhanced the engine with a second panel of pistons. We plan on testing her out this weekend at Sandown Park. It would be wonderful if you and your cousin could come to watch me race," he said.

"That does sound exciting, Mr. Nassar. I do, however, believe that Lady Bergenhalt's dance is this weekend. Perhaps we can plan for the weekend after? I am interested in your improvements and would love to see them in person. Do you have a shop or motor hall you keep the vehicle at? I am sure Nathan would love to see it, as well. He is quite an avid fan, I assure you," I said.

"Oh, of course, how could I forget about the dance? Yes, yes, the following weekend will be just as nice, and young Mr. Starling must attend. If you are so inclined to see the improvements, I can escort you and Starling to our garage next week. Depending on how we do this weekend, there may be some improvements yet to be done."

"A waste of time, if you ask me. Flitting away on a silly racing motor when you could be creating new world improvements. You astound me, brother," Lord Thetford interrupted.

"Oh, brother, can't you see? The improvements we make on the motors can easily be translated to other modes of transportation, you only need to open your mind to see the possibilities. Plus, there is nothing wrong with a little fun. You should try it once in a while."

"When one of your improvements changes the world, I'll eat my watch. And besides, I know plenty of less improvident ways of having fun." He turned towards me with a heated gaze.

"Perhaps brother, you should see to your wife, she seems to be beckoning you," he retorted.

Miro mouthed, "I'm sorry about him," to me, but it did not eliminate the embarrassment creeping up my neck.

As if my anxiety could not rise any further, Constable Weston came bursting through the hall door with a few officers in tow. He made a beeline for me and leaned down to whisper in my ear.

"We've found something." His eyes darted across the table and stared accusingly at Miro.

25

Chapter 25- Coming Off the Rails

When is it time to believe your instincts over your eyes?

I watched in slow motion as the two officers stood opposite me on either side of Miro. Lord Thetford stood up first and objected to whatever possible crime his brother could be accused of. Lady Cornelia Whipley stood and faced Luke in question.

"Nephew, what in God's name is the meaning of this? Why have you brought the law into my lovely luncheon?"

"I apologize, Aunt Cornelia, but there is evidence that cannot be ignored, and we need answers as soon as possible. Mr. Nassar, if you would please come with us, we need to question you post haste," Luke replied.

Miro looked around the room like a rabbit searching for a path of escape, his eyes huge and alarmed. I could scarcely move a muscle as my brain took far too long to catch up.

"I'm not sure what possible reason for this insult can be, but if I can help with resolving a crime, I will." He stood up, exuding more confidence than I knew he felt.

I stood up as well, almost knocking my chair back. "If he is to be interviewed regarding the case we are working on, I shall accompany you."

"Of course, Miss Sweeting, I would not suggest otherwise. Let us leave at once and get some answers," said Luke.

"Miro, don't say a thing, I'll get our lawyer fetched at once. Whatever you've done, don't admit to a thing," said Lord Thetford. His wife clung to his arm, looking pale.

"Thanks for the vote of confidence, brother. I assure you all that I have nothing to hide. Let's go clear my name, constable."

Miro marched out in front of the accompanying officers, his back straight and head forward. Whatever Luke had found, I just couldn't see Miro involved in these crimes. Could he put me in the path of such gore? No. I shook my head at Luke and followed Miro out. This was not right.

We pulled onto a road that contained several motor halls. The one we were to visit was encircled by officers and looky-loos. I saw a silhouette hanging by the corner of the bobby barrier and knew instantly that Nathan was already finding out what had happened. Purgatorio had followed him today instead of accompanying me to the luncheon. I could only wonder what mischief had led them to this garage so quickly. We pulled to the side of the road and got out.

"Well, Miss Sweeting, it looks like you get to see my race motor sooner than anticipated," said Miro, trying to be light-hearted.

"I don't think you want to be voicing that out loud until you see what we've found, Mr. Nassar," Luke said.

"Missus Sweeting, you're here? You'll nawt believe what they've found." Nate sidled up to me with Purgy on his shoulder. He gave Miro a nasty look.

"I don't know what you've been up to sir, but it's nawt good." Nate glared at him.

Miro looked at Nate in confusion as we walked into his garage area.

His gleaming motor sat center stage. There was an array of tools and metal pieces in the surrounding corners. The officers combed through the last of the tool boxes, and Luke directed us to the boot of the motor.

"We received an anonymous note this morning stating that we would find what we were looking for here. It included another piece of the etching the murderer has been leaving with the victims. We were given leave to search from the garage manager you lease from, Mr. Nassar. What can you tell me about the bundle you see here?"

Luke studied Miro as he edged near the boot of the motor. Miro clenched and relaxed his fists with each step. I followed close behind, the curiosity gnawing at my nerves. Looking at the bundle, it didn't seem like much but some cloth tiles. The closer I got, the more I realized that those pieces of fabric were damning, indeed. I gasped at the realization of whose clothes those remnants had been torn from. I looked at Miro with raised brows, and he looked back at me, puzzled.

"What am I supposed to know about some dirty cloths in the back of my motor? There are dirty cloths all around this garage, if you haven't noticed. Full of grease and grime. I would say these are a bit better fabric than my usual shop towels, but…."

Miro picked one up and looked closer. His face paled a bit, and he dropped the fabric quickly.

"Is this what I think it is? It's blood, isn't it? It's that poor girl's blood, and you think I did it? And why wouldn't you, it's in my bloody motor? For all the crown jewels in the kingdom, I have no idea how those got there, constable.

Several people have access to the garage to work on the motor: the cleaning boy Johnny, my partner George Habit, my mechanics, Steven Tabolt and Gregory Callen, and, well, of course, the motor hall manager himself. He has every blooming key there is!" Miro raked his hands through his now disheveled mane and looked from Luke to me and back again.

Purgatorio hissed from Nate's shoulder. "Et tu, Purgy?" Miro said. Luke looked at me.

"What do you think? I need logical Annabelle here. Do not let sentiment cloud your analytical mind," he said.

I looked at Luke hard. I hated and loved that he called me out. I then turned my gaze onto Miro. His green eyes pleaded with me to free him of this dilemma. His reaction did not seem to be an act. I could detect no falsehood in his manners. Although, he had fooled me once before.

"Luke, I don't feel confident that he is to blame. There are just too many clues that don't add up to him. This evidence is quite damning, but with the amount of other people having access, and the nature of it being an anonymous tip has me uneasy. What are your thoughts?"

"I am afraid I have to agree with you. This is just too neat and tidy. Mr. Nassar, I must ask that you don't travel anywhere for the present moment and give me that list of all those who have access to this place that you can think of. I want to know when you recall the last time this boot was opened, and when the last time you were here. If you are innocent, as we are thinking you are, you have to help us prove it. Understood?"

Miro nodded his head in agreement.

"Yes, sir. Whoever set me up is in for a world of pain. I'll need a scrap of parchment and a pencil. I only visit on the weekends, usually to race the motor," he replied.

"I will have an officer tailing you for now. For your own safety, as well as our piece of mind. Plus, whoever is putting you in the spotlight would expect it."

Luke gave the officers final orders to clean up and collect the evidence.

"I want you to follow your schedule like normal, Mr. Nassar. I have a feeling your part isn't quite over in this mystery," said Luke.

One of his officers ran in from the street in a fit.

"Constable Weston, they found him! One-eyed Whitmore nearly drowned. He's been ushered to the hospital, he has. He's not woken up yet," he said.

Luke and I looked at each other, then we dashed out to his motor, leaving Nate and Miro staring after us. We both knew something was about to break.

26

Chapter 26- The Soggy Sage

Fate only plays fair in the theater. Someone break out the thespians!

Before we left the motor hall, Luke gave direction to his lead officer to escort Miro home, and if Nate wanted, him as well. Luke and I raced to the hospital. Purgatorio glided through the sky above us, screeching with excitement. I didn't realize a mechanical myth could get excited, but he looked to be enjoying the chase.

We left Purgatorio outside the front entrance to perform his power recycling. We walked into the front hall of the hospital and were greeted by a lovely, plump nurse named Gilda. She was all in an uproar about the posted officer mucking up her freshly cleaned floor and was none too happy with how they handled the transport for Whitmore.

"You know he has powers, he has? Everyone around here knows it, and he is good to the children. Doesn't have a pence to spare, but gives double to any dough-faced baby he sees. Whitmore kept me from falling flat on my face once. Popped out of nowhere, he did and caught me on a missed stair. He might look rough around the hems, but he is a right good fella. You all should be finding the guy who did this to him instead of haunting his bed like vultures," she said.

"Nurse Gilda, I assure you, I believe in his innocence. He's been a most helpful informant. We are here to watch over him, and make sure no more harm comes to him. He might have vital information on who did this to him, and to those poor girls," I said.

"Oh yes, of course. We cannot see him come to danger in this hospital. You are a sensible girl, I can see that. Well then, back you go. He's in the fourth door on the right. He is still not awake, but the doctor is hopeful."

We thanked her and headed to his room. The halls were quiet except for the buzz of steam-propelled gizmos relaying the patient's vital rhythms. A few whirling bots were dusting the corridors, and one guard posted outside Whitmore's room. I peaked in a few occupied rooms and saw an elderly lady playing chess with a parish nurse apprentice, a leering young gentleman with a broken leg, and an older man who couldn't stop hiccupping. Nothing suggested menace, well perhaps the leering chap, but I didn't think he posed any real threat to our charge.

We passed the guard at the entrance to Whitmore's room with a nod. Shuffling into the small space, we sidled up to his bedside and took a look at the damage. Whitmore's nose was still swollen, and now he had added afflictions. His good eye was puffy and red, his lip broken open, and several deep cuts marred his arms. His head had been bandaged too. He looked a lot worse than when I saw him outside Evanston's.

We waited for the doctor to return, and I edged towards the open window in his room. The air was light and breezy coming through the crack, a rare occasion for the season. I watched the parched trees sway outside in the distance. My eyes drifted to the motor park, and I saw Lady Thetford being let out of the back of her motor. She carried a bouquet and quickened her pace towards the front and out of my view. I turned back towards the bed as the doctor entered the room.

"Well, Miss Sweeting, you managed not to kill one. Good, good."

"Doctor Cannish? I thought you were designated to the dearly departed. You work on the living too, then?"

"Ah, a common misconception. I work on all bodies, Miss Sweeting. I do specialize in the analytics of a corpse and their mysteries, but I do still practice medicine, yes. And, how is our slumbering patient this afternoon? Any sign of waking up yet?"

"We just arrived ourselves, doctor. He has not stirred much," replied Luke.

"Hmmm, indeed."

A loud shout interrupted our conversation, and an argument reached our ears from the front entrance. Someone was not happy with Nurse Gilda.

"What do you mean I can't take these flowers to him? I came all the way to this hovel to see my dear friend and make sure he is okay, and this is the reception I get. This is outrageous! Do you know who I am, who my husband is? He could buy and sell this place tomorrow," shouted Lady Thetford.

"Ma'am, I'm well aware of your standing. I am not subject to your rule though and must follow the proclamations given to me by my superiors. The patient is not to have visitors; in other words, the answer is still no."

The guard outside walked down the hall to Gilda to lend her some support. He, in turn, was subjected to Lady Thetford's rapid-fire scathing remarks.

As the war of words raged down the hall, a shadow on the hallway floor from the opposite end of the corridor crept towards the entrance of our room. The shadow was accompanied by a tinkling of chimes, bells, or metal on metal. One-eye Whitmore's vitals suddenly spiked. His arms and legs began to spasm and flail. Doctor Cannish rushed to his side and shouted to Luke to help restrain the patient. Looking from Whitmore, I returned my gaze to the shadow just outside the door. It was retreating quickly, and I ran towards the door to catch a view of its owner. I looked towards the right, out the door, and saw just the edge of an elbow vanishing around the corner. The shadow headed to the back of the hospital. The shouting down the hall came to an abrupt halt.

"Well then, fine. Make sure he gets these flowers," Lady Thetford sniffed. She left without another word.

I returned to the room and saw One-eyed Whitmore slumbering peacefully once more. For a moment, he reminded me of the story of *Old Man Winkle*.

"He should be okay now, I've given him a sedative and he should be able to answer our questions in a few days. He needs to rest now," said Dr. Cannish.

"Luke, I think you should tell that guard to not leave his post again. No matter what commotion he hears in the front, he needs to remain here. I saw something that bodes ill for Whitmore if he doesn't," I said.

"What did you see?"

"Don't laugh, but I think I just saw the shadow of his fairy from hell. I have a feeling this won't be the last attempt to gain access to this room."

Chapter 27 - Miss Crazy Bloomers

The unraveling of clues is like the unknotting of the fishing line; frustrating at first but oh so satisfying when it's straight again.

The next couple of days went by with no news from Whitmore. Luke was getting impatient, knowing that whatever Whitmore had to say was important to our case. I tried to busy myself with a creation for the dance on Friday.

I spent days in the tinkering room, lost in thought. Nate popped in and out with news of Lord Thetford's attempt to get Miro's officer tail removed. Purgatorio lazed around, waiting for something exciting to happen. Jaime brought me up several meals but left me to my musings. He knew when I was in this mood, it was best to wait for the inevitable breakthrough.

I cut some blood-red fabric and sewed on black lace detail. I then adhered it to a beige corset. I embellished the latches with darkened steel from the smithies. Along the two boning lines on the ribs, I sewed in some loops for storage. The under blouse would be black with red-capped sleeves and black lace trim, just above the elbows. My pantaloons would be black with lavender vertical stripes. The inside of the half-skirt was black, and on the outside, the same blood red as the corset. I poured myself into the work. I didn't want to think about the case, or the death, or the shame of not figuring it out by now.

Anger started to bloom as I pounded some metal gears into feather shapes. Rosy and black hued metals alternating attached to a fierce bird body would wrap my throat. A fiery phoenix choker with red glass eyes stared at me from the table. There is meaning in the pieces I make, and I couldn't help but be fearful of this one. Did this mean I would need to burn before I came out on the other side? Could I handle the heat? I threw down my hammer and left the room. It was clear that whatever the meaning, I needed to face it head-on.

I called the maid for a bath and let the heat soak into my bones as I systematically went through all the detail of the murders I could recall. I knew that both women were servants, and I knew that One-eyed Whitmore was of meager means, as well. I knew that whoever killed those girls had to have been at the dance at the Thetford's that night to steal my brooch from Jaime's coat pocket. I knew from One-eye that my suspicions of being targeted were correct by his vein of information in the Brass Boroughs. The upper servants were definitely spreading information at Tappers.

Was one of the servants involved? Angry with their employer? Had I slighted them somehow? Jealousy, maybe? No, that wasn't it. Lord Thetford was seen inspecting the gears of the coat rack right before Gwen was found in the closet looking at the floor. Think, Annabelle, think!

Katherine Hayes had been pregnant when she died. The father of the baby was said to be of high society. Someone out of her league. And, why was Mr. Cosswald trailing her about that night? He and that damn bell were there. The bell, like the tinkling of hell fairies. The sound I heard in the hospital was different, though.

It was on the tip of my brain. I plunged my head below the water's surface in hopes of clarity. I held my breath until I heard a pounding outside the tub. Breaking the surface, I looked to find the nature of the noise. Pounding resumed in the form of knocking at my chamber door.

"I'm in the bath, who is it?"

"Cousin, it's me. I thought I better inform you we're leaving in half an hour. I know that you sometimes get lost in thought. Are you okay?"

I chuckled at Jaime yelling through the door.

"Cousin, have you gone mad? I hear laughter. You're not laughing at me, are you?"

That had me cackling hysterically.

"Well, Miss Crazy Bloomer, do hurry up or we will miss all the fun!"

I could hear him stomping away. A smile remained on my lips as I left the bath and rushed to get dressed. The maid came in to help me with the final touches. I placed the beautiful amethyst hairpin in my freshly coiffed hair and adjusted the ruby dagger bracer to my right forearm. I fastened the phoenix choker necklace and stood silent. I felt like I was preparing for battle. I suppose in society, that is what a young lady does when one is headed to a dance like this. I buckled up my black and gray boots and took one more look in the mirror.

Another knock came from my door. It was quite persistent, and I opened it to find my cousin standing there. He stepped back in surprise at the sudden opening of the door. He silently assessed me and rotated his finger in the air in an unspoken direction for me to twirl for him. I did and smirked at his expression.

"I don't know if you're Lust or Wrath cousin, but I'm jealous! Or should I say, Envious? I'm glad I wore the green tonight.

"Thank you, Jaime. I think I can safely say, I am Wrath. And if anyone tries to ruin my night with either murder or mayhem, they will feel it."

28

Chapter 28- Dance of Distraction

The world spins and dips me like an over enthusiastic dance partner. Ouch, my toe!

I wasn't sure what I expected when I arrived at the Bergenhalt's, but whatever it was, my imagination could never compare to the real thing. Motor attendants waited as the line of vehicles curled around the half-moon driveway. They were dressed in suits styled with flame lapels and smoky black fabric. Top hats of black with fiery brims were angled sideways on their heads. Clocks, only numbering up to 7, ticked along on their shoulders. The entrance to the residence had similar adornments. It looked like you were entering the gates of hell.

My cousin and I stepped out of our motor. Nathan and Purgatorio emerged from the other side, decked out with top hats embellished with fake coins and banknotes. My "greedy" little companions made quite the pair. Our group walked up the stairway and into the entrance hall. There were several doorways each leading to a different sin. The first, the parlor, guarded by a servant laying in an armchair with one leg over an arm, clearly led to Sloth. His hair, styled messy and wayward, made me smile. The servant gave me a cheeky wink back as he caught me staring.

The second doorway led to the dining room. A robust woman with a fruit hat and a decanter of wine lounged outside it on a chaise. She invited guests in to sample the delicious treats the kitchen had prepared. Gluttony was definitely a room I was looking forward to entering. Food was one of my favorite sins, and, oh, the smells that were wafting out were, dare I say, heavenly. Nathan left us immediately for that room, with Purgy perched on his shoulder.

The third doorway, leading to the library, was posted with a servant outfitted in cards. Peering in, I could see several tables already heavily populated by the men of society. Cards in hand, they wagered in hopes of winning the night. Greed was definitely a favorite among them.

A woman with the finest silks and jewelry angled herself in a regal pose outside the drawing room door. Another woman with clearly outdated fashions stood opposite her. She looked longingly at the woman and into the room at the lavish decorations and tea services. *The grass is always greener* tumbled through my mind. They were both completely in character. The Proud woman looked me up and down as I passed and looked back at herself. A smile creased her lips, and she lifted her nose in the other direction. The Envious lady tried to copy her pose, I chuckled.

The last doorway led to the ballroom. It appeared to be split down the middle. A gentleman in black with a wicked mustache stood to the left, while a lady in a faux nude bodice with dark wine lacing and a hip slit wine skirt stood on the right looking sultry. He looked heatedly at her as she flirted with every man that walked past. Jaime and I walked closer towards the couple before realizing they were our hosts.

"Lord and Lady Bergenhalt, your party is by far the best of the season, if not the century! Let us compliment you on your amazing decor and costumes," Jaime said.

"Yes, quite splendid. I agree with my cousin wholeheartedly. I have never seen the like." I looked around the ballroom. The band played a tango, and the hired dancers floated around the room with an equal amount of rage and desire as the guests looked on. The guests waited with excitement for their own dancing to begin.

"Oh, you are both so kind. Yes, I will admit it takes a whole year to plan, but it is truly delightful. My dear husband and I both just love the theatrics of it all. Don't we, Daniel?"

"Yes, dear. I do enjoy anything I do with you." He winked at her.

"I must say, Miss Sweeting, you could be a part of the troupe, for sure. Your necklace is quite stunning," Lady Bergenhalt said.

My hand instantly touched the cold metal of the phoenix.

"Thank you so much. I made it myself. I poured a little Wrath into hammering these wings, I assure you."

That earned me a chuckle.

"Well, perhaps next year, I might call on you for some ideas or better yet, pieces, if you're willing to part with some."

"Oh cousin, you must! I know you planned on getting into the fashion business, but I think your gizmos and baubles are the rage all the ton has been waiting for."

"You know, I think you might be right, Jaime. Lady Bergenhalt, I would be honored if you considered some of my pieces for your next party. Once you have a theme, do let me know, and I will put some things together," I replied.

She clapped her hands together, and her husband looked adoringly at her glee.

"Excellent! We must get back to our roles now, but I will reach out when we do have a theme in mind."

They turned from us and picked up their angered lover act for the other guests passing by.

My cousin and I entered the ballroom to catch the end of the tango. It was mesmerizing, watching the couple twirl and dip with passionate glances. The eyelash flutters, the caressed jawline, the hips swaying in sync were all very, well, sinful. I giggled to myself. Jaime gave me a strange look, and I just shook my head.

The song ended, and the gas lighting brightened in the room, the atmosphere changing to a more suitable element.

"Oh cousin, don't look now, but I think it happened again. If that isn't a sign, I don't know what is," Jaime said.

"What do you mean, cousin?"

"Lady Whipley and *your* constable just walked in the ballroom, and my, oh my."

I looked toward the direction he indicated and took in a breath. Lady Cornelia Whipley was dressed in a golden ensemble complete with a headdress. She looked like a Greek goddess or a golden statue of one. Quite lovely. Beside her stood Luke, his eyes scanning the room and stopping when they collided with mine.

He wore a black bowler hat tilted just off-center, a pair of red and steel goggles wrapped around the hatband. A black leather one-shoulder chest harness, fitted to perfection, rested on a blood red shirt with a black embroidered Celtic design woven throughout. His strong legs were in a pair of black pantaloons, and his black boots were covered in matching red belted spats. He wore two short leather bracers on each forearm.

As he walked towards me with Lady Whipley on his arm, I felt the pang of envy hit me, and it wasn't my cousin next to me.

"Belle, you are in so much trouble! Lucky you," Jaime whispered.

"Ah, Lady Whipley, I can't tell if you're Greed or Pride, but I am envious, both in outfit and in truth. You look ravishing, dear," he said.

"Oh, Mr. Nethersby, you are such a flatterer. I love that shade of green on you. This needle work is amazing," she gushed as she looked closer at his vest.

The conversation continued like the constant buzz of a beehive. I continued to stare at Luke and him at me. He finally broke the spell with a voice a bit more gravelly than usual.

"Well, Miss Sweeting, it seems we are a matched set once again. Do you think it would be safe to combine our rage for a dance or five?"

I blushed, my lips curled into a grin at his words.

"I'll chance it if you will, Constable Weston."

He took my hand as the band signaled the next set. He slowly twirled me into position. The music began, and our opposite hands touched in the center as we moved in a circle. We switched hands and went the opposite way. We broke apart and went around the next couple in line to join our hands once again.

The longing that this room evoked filled me as we danced across the floor. Luke's hand touched my lower back when we glided into another turn. I felt its heated impression long after it left to join my hand again.

His eyes mirrored mine as we stared at one another. Losing ourselves in the moment, the music, the sin.

We forewent decorum and stayed paired for the waltz that followed. He held me close, twirling like a pair on top of a music box. My face was flushed and rosy from some unknown heat that crept up my neck. His eyes were dark pools of molten chocolate swimming with an emotion I didn't quite understand but delighted me. I wanted to stay in this oasis, this little slice of hell that resembled heaven. The waltz ended. He took my hand, and we drifted out of the ballroom. We walked oblivious to the other guests, sharing smiles and hidden arm touches as we moved. He directed us to the dining hall, where we sampled fruit tarts, braised pork, and a delightful sherry that went straight to my head.

Well, that is what I told myself, drifting through the night like a wisp through the woods. We took turns picking a new room to explore. Some sins were decorated to be silly, some to be festive, and some to induce sin. Greed was a very good one for that.

We ended up in the ballroom again and circled the edge of the space watching the couples in the current dance line. Miss Cara Cosswald danced with Jaime, her face betraying her excitement. Miss Whitney Cosswald was dancing with Lord Thetford. Lady Whipley danced with a gentleman I did not know, and Lady Thetford was dancing with Miro. I just realized I hadn't seen him all night, and I also realized that I didn't mind. I looked over toward Luke and smiled. He grinned back and tugged at a loose lock of my hair.

"Have I told you that you look incredible tonight? Because, if I haven't, Belle, I assure you that no other could compare."

"Thank you, Luke. You cut quite a striking figure, as well," I replied.

I touched his shoulder armor and dragged a finger down the beveled detailing. Luke moved closer and traced the phoenix feather along my collar bone, gently brushing my skin. He left tingles in his wake.

"Shall we dance again?"

I nodded, and he led me out onto the floor.

The music began to play, and before we could move into step, a boisterous voice penetrated our bubble.

"Ah, Constable Weston, you don't mind, do you? I must dance with this lovely creature at once! You've been hogging her far too long as it is."

Not waiting for confirmation, Lord Oliver Thetford grabbed my hand and pulled me into the dance with him. Wrath just may make an appearance after all.

29

Chapter 29- Heaven Help Me

I will not scream at an earl. I will not scream at an earl.

Lord Thetford maneuvered us as far away from Luke as he could. Luke looked as angry as I felt. He couldn't make his way through the crush, and I could tell was resigned to not make a scene.

"Oh, none of that, Miss Sweeting. You know you need to switch partners, or the whole of society will be gossiping. Besides, if we are to be better familiarized with each other, there is nothing better than a dance."

He twirled me about and caught me at the waist. I felt imprisoned in his strong arms.

"You are quite the talk of the ton already, I'd say. And for good reason, Annabelle. I can call you Annabelle, right? And you will call me Oliver. Yes, I think we are quite well acquainted and will be even more in the future."

His self-assured attitude had my stomach in knots.

"Lord Thetford, I am not sure what you mean by that, but I feel that it would be inappropriate to call you by your Christian name. We've only met a handful of times, and you are married."

As if summoning her from the ether, Lady Thetford was at the edge of the dance floor shooting daggers at us with her eyes.

"Oh, come now. I've heard you call my brother by his name. You can surely do the same with me. I think we shall be great friends," he replied. He decreased the gap between us as he said 'great friends'.

"May I cut in?"

"Oh God, yes!"

I didn't even know who it was, but I was desperate to get away from this smug, entitled earl. He gave a bit of resistance, giving the gentleman behind me a withering look that would set most men down. Lord Thetford relented, however, as he took in the watching eyes of society. I turned into the waiting arms of Miro. He smiled shyly and spun me around to the music. He moved like a panther, smooth and graceful.

"Good evening, Annabelle. I wasn't sure if I would see you tonight, but I'm glad you are here."

"Why wouldn't I be here?" It came out harsher than I intended, the earl's unwanted advances still in my mind.

"Not you, I wasn't sure if I was going to attend. The last few days have been quite hellish. I am trying to do stuff as normal. But to know a killer was in my motor hall, and trying to frame me, has me most anxious," he replied.

I softened towards his admission.

"Yes, it has been a trying time, indeed. I am glad you are here, as well. Are you still racing tomorrow?"

"No, it's been postponed to Sunday. They realized most of the regulars with any coin would be attending this party, so they wanted to give them time to recuperate."

"Oh well, that is a sound idea. Will you be driving?"

"I will be. Would you... I mean if you're not otherwise engaged, can you make it?"

Hope flared in his green eyes. He was still my friend, and I wanted to support him. Especially now, when the world seemed to be setting him up as the scapegoat.

"Yes, I think I will be able to attend," I said.

He picked me up and twirled me around as the song ended. As he set me down, an angry constable stood beside us.

"Mr. Nassar, I am surprised to see you here. I would think you would be staying at home, playing it safe," Luke said gruffly.

"You did tell me to proceed as normal, constable, and this is a party that I would never miss. I thank you for your concern, though," he replied. A touch of sarcasm betrayed his countenance.

"Yes, I did, didn't I?" Luke rubbed his hand through the slight stubble that had surfaced on his face over the last few days. "And if I heard right, you will be racing this Sunday?"

"You don't miss a thing. Yes, that is correct, and Miss Annabelle has just agreed to accompany me," Miro smiled.

"Has she, indeed?" Luke looked at me with a raised eyebrow.

"I have, Constable Weston." I looked at him with an air of challenge. "Besides, if we want to catch this killer, what better way than at the motor races. We know that they have access to Mr. Nassar's hall, we know that in all likelihood they will be there plotting to ingrain the belief deeper that he is to blame. Perhaps we could even catch them in the act of planting more evidence?"

Luke looked at me in awe, his eyes softening as he took in my words.

"You do amaze me sometimes, Belle. That is a very sound idea. What say you, Mr. Nassar? You want to be our bait?"

"I was going to be at the races anyway, and if it helps put this whole horrid affair behind me, I am more than willing," he said.

"What's this about the races? You're still doing that, are you brother?"

Lord and Lady Thetford sidled up beside us, interjecting themselves into the conversation.

"Yes, brother. Constable Weston and Miss Sweeting will be attending this Sunday. They think it will be a great way to…." I nudged him in the side with my elbow and shook my head. He nods, getting my understanding. "They think it will be a great time, and best to put some normalcy back in my routine. They are still keeping a close eye on me, it seems," he finished.

Lord Thetford gave Luke a look of pure disdain, and Lady Thetford just nodded her head.

"I don't know which one of you is trying to drag our name through the mud, but it is quite vexing," Lord Thetford said, looking between Miro and Luke.

"If Miss Sweeting is going, then Talia and I must attend as well. Isn't that right, dear? I suppose it would be best to see how my brother's time is wasted if he will be carted off to prison any day now."

"Oh Oliver, you are so volatile. I am sure it is much like the horse races your father took you to as a child. You enjoyed those. You still talk of them often," Lady Thetford said.

"Ah, I suppose you are right, dearest. It might not be terrible after all. Yes, we shall make a day of it. What say you, Miss Sweeting?"

"I will be attending with Mr. Nethersby and Nathan Starling. Constable Weston, will you be with us as well?"

"I will stay close to Mr. Nassar. He has offered to show me the inner workings of the latest motors," Luke replied.

"Ah yes, indeed. Of course, you and Starling are invited to see the mechanics before the race as well, Miss Sweeting," said Miro.

We finalized our plans for the upcoming race, and I went in search of Jaime and Nathan to discuss the event. I found my cousin in the Pride/Envy room sharing a tea service with Lord Cosswald. Every time the lord laughed, the bell jingled in his pocket. I eyed him suspiciously as I neared the table. I couldn't shake the idea of One-eyed Whitmore and his fairies from hell

"Lord Cosswald, how are you this evening?"

"Ah, Miss Sweeting, I am just delighted with your cousin. He is quite a riot. It is quite refreshing, after I lost so dreadfully in the Greed room. Lady Cosswald will have my head later, for sure, " he joked.

"Sir, do you by chance know One-eyed Whitmore?"

His eyes flashed with trepidation. "Why do you ask, Miss Sweeting?"

"Oh, I was just thinking about him and how he is laid up in the hospital still unconscious," I said.

He relaxed at that and replied, "Ah Whitmore, poor fellow. I know of him but can't say that we are on familiar terms. All that mumbo-jumbo gives me the willies. I'm kind of glad he is off the streets. Don't want that riffraff around my girls, you know?"

"Surely he isn't bad, Lord Cosswald?" Jaime interjected.

"In fact, I've heard he's helped many a person in his way."

"Well, he can keep his help far away from me."

He stood then, bowed to us both, and made an excuse of needing to find Lady Cosswald.

Jaime and I shared a look and then searched for Nathan and Purgatorio so we could head home. We found the duo in the Sloth Room. Nate was laid out on a chair with a full belly, and Purgy was recharging in the corner. Nate scurried up when he noticed us standing above him.

"Ah missus, sorry 'bout that. Are we ready to go then? What a Glimmer of a party, hey, missus? I swear I've never seen the like. Took me all my willpower not to snitch an item or five. But, I didn't, I swear it," he said.

"Well, I am glad of that, Nathan Starling! Lady Bergenhalt might hire me to make some pieces for her next year, and I daresay she will dismiss the thought entirely if my guest is pilfering her home."

"I was only jesting, miss! I promised ya that I would be good, and I aim to keep it," he replied.

"You best, young sir," Jaime chimed in.

"Okay, off we go, we need to discuss a few things on the way home, Nate. We have quite the plan brewed up for Sunday, and I'll need you at your best," I said.

"Oh yeah, missus? I do love me a good scheme."

We collected Purgatorio and headed out into the night.

30

Chapter 30- Meeting of Minds

Like the pieces of a stained glass window, I needed to see the whole, not just the fragments.

The following day I took out my notebook and studied the clues we'd uncovered so far. Before we left the dance, I asked Luke to come by in the afternoon with the pieces of etched paper we had found in the hands of the victims. I hadn't given them enough thought. Something about last night's theme and the memory of those pieces gave me an inkling that they needed to be explored more deeply.

Word had gotten around the Bergenhalt party that the race at Sandown Park would be the next must-attend event. I wasn't too thrilled that Lord and Lady Thetford invited themselves into our group, but it would be social suicide to slight them. I tried to not be distracted by the uncomfortable thought.

Refocusing on my notes, I replayed the scenes in my head.

Posed as dancers, throats cut by a weak, left-handed assailant. Items left in both hands deliberately, and both relating to me. Did we ever find out if Gwen had anything on her leg too? I must remember to ask Luke when he arrives. Both were killed sometime in the night or early morning. How does Whitmore equate into it? He said he didn't know or see anything, but that must not be the case. I wish he would wake up and tell us who attacked him! Someone was in the hallway at the hospital. Why was Lady Thetford there? I needed to ask her at the race. Who put the evidence in Miro's motor boot, and why would they want to frame him?

I tapped the end of my pencil to my chin. I needed more pieces. A knock on the library door brought me back to the present. Luke came in with a stack of notebooks. He slung them down onto the table I was working on, as a way of greeting. I smiled up at him.

"I find your studious look quite appealing, Miss Sweeting. Any momentous breakthroughs this morning?"

"Well, Constable Weston, I seem to be missing some key elements so I am very glad you are here."

"I see. So you're only glad I'm here for my notes, hey? How disappointing," he teased.

I flushed at the fervid look in his eyes. Luke broke his heated gaze and shook his head. He sat down and fanned out his paperwork in preparation for our mission; to connect some puzzling pieces in this narrative.

"Where do you want to start, Belle?"

"Did Gwen Vannery have a mark on her leg similar to the violinist?"

"Yes, but it was two lines. That's not the interesting part, though."

I looked at him in anticipation.

"Whitmore has three lines on his leg. Doctor Cannish just sent over a report to me this morning after discovering it," he said.

"The simplest answer is usually the correct one. It's a count, perhaps Roman numerals, or just lines. We wouldn't know unless there was a fourth victim, I'd say."

"Yes, that is what I was thinking, as well," Luke said.

I smirked at him.

"What?"

"Oh, nothing. How is Whitmore? Did Doctor Cannish give any inclination as to when he will be awake?"

"No, he did say his levels are all back to normal, but it seems something is blocking him. I don't think we should count on him to solve this. I want you to stay close to your cousin tomorrow, okay? I will be down by the motor hall with Mr. Nassar watching for anything out of sorts, and I need you to be safe," Luke said.

"Yes, yes, and Nate will be with me, as well as Purgatorio. I need them both to fend off the terrible Lord Thetford."

"What do you mean, did he accost you?" The suspicion in his eyes turned to something hostile as he waited for my answer.

"No, no, but he gives me the creeps, and he does insinuate things. He makes me uneasy."

"We'll have to have a conversation, him and I. I don't like you feeling this way. He may be wealthy, but he doesn't have the right to take what's mine."

"What's yours? I'm yours now, am I? When did this happen?"

He backpedaled a bit. "What I meant is, you're under my protection as a colleague and friend and maybe soon something more, and I won't have you feeling hunted by the likes of someone like him," he said firmly.

I felt tingly all over at the declaration. Luke clearly took this protector thing farther than I anticipated, and I liked it. I met his eyes, and a slow smile spread across my face. He returned my grin.

"Uh hem, let's see. Do you have those etching pieces?"

"Yes, right here. Again, Doctor Cannish found one in Whitmore's pocket. So, clearly, he was meant to die. How he got away, I'm not sure," he said.

"If he would only wake up, we could ask him," I sighed.

We put the four pieces in front of us. The first, from Katherine, had a "T" on it, the second, from Gwen, had an "A" on it, the third, from the bundle found in Miro's garage, depicted no letters on it, and the fourth, from Whitmore, was water-logged and smudged. The letter could have been an "H"or another "A". I wasn't sure. That was not what made me go stock still.

"Oh, my gracious!" I rearranged the piece to make the etching connect more. "I know where this is from!"

I rushed to the bookshelf and pulled out my cousin's copy of Dante's Inferno.

"I can't believe I didn't see it before! Right in my face."

"Belle, I don't understand, what is it?"

I flipped through the tome in search of the page I needed.

"Here, Luke! Here it is! It's this picture right here. It's the top left corner of Botticelli's illustration of the circles of hell…. Huh."

"What's huh?"

"Well, you see here? It's the entrance to hell on the hill, but then these other pieces completely skip limbo and go straight to the second circle," I said.

"Well, what's the second circle?"

My eyes met his with a mix of concern and revelation.

"Luke, the second circle of hell is Lust."

31

Chapter 31- Off to the Races

"The gates of hell are open night and day; smooth the descent, and easy is the way." -Virgil

I tossed and turned in bed that night. My mind produced images of tortured bodies tumbling about, caught in storms of their own making. Was the murderer punishing these women because they were lustful, or was the murderer lusting after them? And what did these clues have to do with me?

Waking up from a restless sleep, I struggled to untangle my legs from the blankets. The closer we got to the answer, the more questions piled up. A mountain of mystery I wasn't sure I wanted to surmount. What if I didn't like what I found on the other side? Based on what I've already deduced, I can say that would be guaranteed.

I stretched my arms above me and moved my head side to side to work the kinks from my neck. Whatever today would bring, I wanted to be prepared. I launched out of bed and wet my face with the water bowl set out in my room. Steam rolled up around me as the cloth of hot water made contact with my face. My dark brown hair looked black on the ends along my face, where the water had been absorbed.

I walked toward the looking glass and scanned my reflection. There was a tightness in my eyes that wasn't there at the beginning of the season. The strain was evident from the unexpected darkness that clouded my recent days. There was lightness too, though. Gorgeous vibrant scenes of new friendships, possibilities, and perhaps love. I caught myself smiling and turned to get ready for the day.

I walked down to the breakfast room in a lavender vested bodice with silver detailing. I chose to forgo a skirt entirely and replaced it with a pair of leather belted pants that taper towards the ankles. On my waist sat several angled belts equipped with shaped pockets and compartments for my pocket change, extra bobby pins, a small notebook, buttons, and a few odds and ends I thought I might need. My dark leather calf boots clasped up with shiny silver latches. The same leather was used for my fingerless half gloves, which adorned my hands. I had on my red gem-encrusted dagger bracer from Whitmore, and the hairpin from Nate was tucked firmly in a high bun. I felt ready to take on the world.

Nate was filling his plate at the sideboard, and Jaime was reading the paper in the breakfast room. He folded the top corner back at my entrance.

"Well, cousin, are you ready for the races today? It should be quite good sport. Young Starling has been buzzing since he came down," Jaime said.

"I do hope it isn't spoiled by any murders."

The room went silent. Nate and Jaime stared at me in horror.

"Seriously gentlemen, I just don't think I can take another shock. But then again, I just want this mystery solved so we can give those girls some peace. The longer it goes on, the more I feel like a failure," I admitted.

"Oh, Belle, this is your very first attempt, did you really think it would be that easy? "

"No, of course not."

"I know you feel these deaths more acutely with your tender heart. I love you all the more for your empathetic nature, but without experience, some things you won't solve. So, do what you do best. Follow the clues, listen to people, and observe. I know you and the constable will work this out, and if you are right, something will happen today. You must be careful, and not put yourself in a compromising position, okay?"

"Yes, cousin. Besides, I will be in the audience with you, and Nathan will be nearby," I replied.

A chuff from the side interjected.

"And you as well, Purgatorio." I paused for a moment. "The person I really fear for is Mr. Nassar. Luke will be watching over him, but if these criminals want to get to him, what better way than in a crowded raceway."

"Well if Luke is watching over him, I would say he is quite safe, indeed. Unless he means to knock out the competition!"

"Oh Jamie, you do love to needle me!"

"Aw right you two. Get to eatin' then. We have a race to go to, and I aim to win me a bit more coin," Nate said.

"Oh really, Starling? Are you a gambling aficionado now? Perhaps I should give you a bit to wager for me," Jaime said.

"Nawt sure what an aficanago is, but I've had a bit of a luck run recently. You let me know if you're wanting in, sir. I'm not claiming to be nothin' special, but I know where the hot bets are."

It looked like these two were going to get into a different kind of trouble today. We finished our plates and prepared to depart. Stewart helped me put my light jacket on and patted my shoulder gently.

"Be careful today. We've all grown quite fond of you, milady."

Shocked by his admission, all I could do was nod. It almost felt like I was being sent to face the trials of Hercules. What a strange idea, indeed. We sped away from Bread Street. Some of us in search of riches, and others needed answers.

153

32

Chapter 32- Start Your Motors

"But to return, and view the cheerful skies, in this the task and mighty labor lies."

  -Virgil

The buzz of excitement was catching as we entered the gates of the racing park. Mechanical beasts, like Purgy, were flying about the stands bringing patrons refreshments. It appeared Miro had found a market for his creations already. A shiny harpy fluttered past us, and Purgy startled her with a roar. Luckily, she didn't drop her goods from her talons, or it would have been quite the mess. A booth selling fanciful extending binoculars adjoined one selling roasted hazelnuts. The smells made my mouth water even though I had just finished breakfast.

Jaime handed Nathan some money.

"Okay, young Starling, go make me rich, or at the very least, don't lose it all." He winked at Nate.

"Nathan, don't forget your other quest while you are here. I need you to stay in Miro's temporary motor hall while the race is happening. Stay out of sight, and watch your back," I said.

"Yes, missus. I will, indeed. No one is better at staying hidden than me. Well, I guess unless we count that time at the train station, but I was off that day. I'll go and get this wagering done and meet you afterward, before the race."

Nate nodded and took off to find his bookmaker for his and my cousin's bets. I shook my head, smiling. Jaime just gave me a shoulder shrug in return. Purgatorio stayed perched on my shoulder today, his eyes looking this way and that, in search of some unknown threat. His metal hackles shivered as Lord Thetford approached. I'm pretty sure mine would, too, if I had some.

"Talia, over here. I've found them," he shouted behind him.

Lady Thetford appeared at his elbow shortly after, and her servant Callen scurried away, upon her direction. She watched my eyes follow him. You could really see a difference in how my cousin treated his staff compared to the elite Thetfords. It made me pity Callen.

"Ah, Miss Sweeting, we've been waiting forever. We have a lovely box to watch the race from. Did you know that this motor track is not oval at all, but oddly shaped? There are many twists and turns to keep the drivers on their toes. Such fun!" She clapped her hands together and led me toward our reserved box seating. Lord Thetford flanked me on the other side.

"My brother, I guess, does have a point. This racing business appears to be quite fun, as he puts it. What say you, Miss Sweeting?"

We walked out to the balcony we would be viewing the race from, and my breath caught. The motor course gleamed in the sunlight, coiling this way and that, like a serpent eating its own tail. The shiny motors, parked along the outer edge of the track near the driving tunnels, were getting one last look through before racing started. I saw Miro down by his motor, and he looked up and waved. He beckoned me to come down by him.

Purgatorio and I squeezed out from between the Thetfords, and I grabbed Jaime's hand. I offered my apologies for abruptly leaving to the Thetfords, and I told them we would be back shortly. We met Nate in the hall and followed the tunnel out, where Miro was preparing. He smiled at our approach, and Purgy took off towards the sky above the track.

"It's a great day for racing, Miss Sweeting. Even better, now that you're here," he said. He took my hand and brushed his lips upon my knuckles. I smiled.

"Thank you, Mr. Nassar, you are too kind. It does appear to be ideal weather. Can we see the engine, or do you have to start lining up?"

"Ah, please, sir, can we? I nawt see one before, and I am bleaming begging!" exclaimed Nate.

"Right, Starling and Sweeting, I believe there is just enough time for a looksie."

Miro smiled with pride. His manner was all ease and comfort as he guided us towards the front of his motor. Propelled gizmos buzzed through the air around us, tightening bolts and polishing windows.

"You see here, it's all tip-top. My mechanic, Steven, was up all night tinkering, making sure it was ready to go. Gregory came in just this morning to take a look as well. He is a bit of a perfectionist, and loves things elegant and in order. Strange for a man of his standing. Look at the tubing here. It adds an accelerant to the fuel to give me a little kick along the straighter paths, and this bob here pushes out a plume of steam so it doesn't overheat," he said excitedly.

"Gregory seems like an interesting fellow. I don't believe I've met him yet," I said.

"Well, of course, you have. Gregory Callen, he goes by Callen, usually. He is Talia's servant, and he has been with her family for years, since before she married Oliver. Callen works on my motor on the side for some extra coin. I can't blame him really, my brother is a miser when it comes to money. Unless it promotes the business," he said.

An air of unease washed over me. My gut compelled me to say, "I don't think you should race today. It doesn't seem safe."

He pointed to his chest. "This gear I'm wearing is made from thick, fire-treated leather. Several layers have been forged together and coated with a special oil cooked into the material. It is very strong and durable. My helmet is lined with the same leather, and the outer shell is made of the toughest metal imaginable. It's lightweight, of course. Your acquaintance, Charles Kaplan, worked it up for me. So, I will be just fine"

"Wicked!" Nate reached out and touched the leather chest gear with reverence. I reached out a hand to feel the texture as well. I heard a throat clear behind me and turned to find Luke.

"Oh, Constable Weston! I was wondering where you were. Did Mr. Nassar tell you about this wonderful material he is wearing? I understand it is quite durable, indeed," I rambled on.

"Miss Sweeting, you look radiant today. He did not mention his clothes to me, but that is indeed fascinating," he said.

He bent forward, took my hand, and kissed the top. His eyes looked up towards me in the most scintillating manner. I felt my cheeks grow hot.

"I will be on the sidelines down here watching the stands and racers for any suspicious activities. You will be in the box with an eagle eye view. Young Starling, we know where you'll be, yes?"

"Yes, sir. I'm heading that way now that the race is 'bout to start," Nate replied

"Nathan, what motor shall I be cheering on?" Jaime asked before Nathan dashed off.

"Oh yes, Mr. Nethersby, I done forgot. You'll be hollering for that shiny red one over there," he said.

"What, not Mr. Nassar's?"

"Ah sir, well, I've done the digging, and he hasn't won one yet, always second or third. Red over there is due for another win today. It looks good by all accounts, sir."

"Harsh, young Starling, but you are correct," Miro said. "We were hoping to make today the first win, so while I'd hate for you to lose your money, I hope you do so," he jested.

Nate blushed a bit at that. He tipped his hat and headed towards the tunnel. Jaime and I wished Miro luck and headed back to our seats.

The motors lined up, staggered across the trackway. Hearty cheers sounded from the Brass stands as the engines revved. The Glimmers, as Nate called them, were too dignified for that. They clapped their gloved hands, with their heads held high, in a more acceptable manner. I chuckled to myself at the ridiculousness of it all. Even at the same event, people of society needed to make their superiority known.

A thought popped into my head just then. I turned to Lady Thetford and asked, "Talia, I saw you at the hospital the other day trying to bring One-eyed Whitmore some flowers. I was wondering how you knew him?"

"You must be mistaken, Miss Sweeting. I was not at the hospital," she replied, her face paling.

"Lady Thetford, there is no mistake. You had a most vivid encounter with the front desk nurse."

She was about to reply when the starting gun sounded. The motors took off at breakneck speeds. The momentary distraction allowed Lady Thetford to engage the person on her right in conversation, completely boxing me out. Lord Thetford leaned in.

"Miss Sweeting, she doesn't talk about it much, but my wife was schoolmates with Whitmore. They were quite good friends until he gave her one of his crazy visions. She hasn't told me what it was exactly, but it made her quite upset," said Lord Thetford.

My mouth formed an 'O' at that, and I looked back at Talia. She was purchasing some beverages from a miniature mechanical centaur. Lord Thetford followed my gaze.

"We've got quite a business deal with those creatures at events like this. They don't need breaks, can handle heavy loads, and people seem to love the novelty. What do you think of our little myths, Annabelle? By the way you and that manticore stick together, I'd say you are an admirer."

"Yes, Lord Thetford, they are wondrous inventions! Your brother and you have quite the knack for creation," I replied.

"I told you, call me Oliver."

Lady Thetford moved towards us then, with drinks in hand.

"Mr. Nethersby, you must try this, it is so very refreshing!" Lady Thetford maneuvered between us to hand Jaime a fruity-looking cocktail. "It's the most delightful thing, full of lavender and fresh berries," she continued.

"Ah, why thank you, Lady Thetford." Jaime took a big gulp and nodded his agreement. "Quite delicious, indeed! Cousin, would you like a sip?"

"Oh, no! That is for you, sir. I can get Miss Sweeting one as well. No need to share," Talia said.

I assured her that was unnecessary, as I was not currently thirsty. The motors were making their second of three laps, and I looked on for Miro's vehicle. Just like Nathan had said, it was lingering between third and fourth place. I watched as Miro maneuvered for a better position. A groan sounded from behind me, and I turned to find Jaime clenching his stomach.

"My dear cousin, I am not feeling very well. I think I better visit the privy." He whispered in my ear and hurried out of the box.

"Is everything okay, Miss Sweeting?" Lady Thetford looked at me with concern and something else while she clung to her husband's arm.

"He said he had a bit of a sour stomach. He should return shortly," I replied.

I signaled for Purgatorio to fly down and join me in the box. An unease was creeping over me, and I wanted someone, or rather something I trusted to be by my side.

The motors rounded a curve to a straightaway that would lead to the finish. Miro's motor lurched forward, as I guessed he hit that accelerant button of his, and then came the most horrid thunderous boom. I looked on in shock. The front of his motor exploded, sending him into a death spin. His vehicle hit the track wall hard. The crowd went silent for a moment, then chaos.

33

Chapter 33- Utter Chaos

Chaos is merely a series of events out of order. It makes one most discombobulated.

The first voice to break the silence was a wailing scream from Lady Thetford. Then, like dominoes, the crowd fell to hysterics. Lady Thetford fainted into Lord Thetford's arms. People crushed closer to the wall to see the scene in all its fiery wreckage. Purgatorio took flight and circled the crash below. I watched Luke dash to Miro's motor, trying to tame the flames with the flail of his coat. Miro's hand reached out the window towards him. Luke and other racers worked to pry the door open to release him. Fuel pooled out the bottom and formed a trail towards them. They needed to move faster before it caught fire.

Using a bar from a lever apparatus, Luke wedged the door open. Miro roared as they tried to free him. His leg appeared to be smashed below the wheel. Luke used the bar again, and while he held the collapsed motor console up, the men pulled Miro out. Luke let go and ran as the trail of fuel ignited, sending scorching heat in his direction. Captivated by the scene below, I barely registered Lady Thetford being escorted out by Callen. Lord Thetford took my elbow and guided me toward the back of the box. I followed without resistance, and we moved through the crush to the tunnel entrance.

"Callen is seeing Talia home, we must see how my brother fares. Are you up for it, Miss Sweeting?" He shouted over the crowd.

I nodded my head, and we quickly made our way to the track. A hospital wagon was already being admitted to the motor entrance as we came to stand by Luke.

"How is he? Do we know what the damage is?" Lord Thetford had a look of concern that I'd never seen him display before.

"It looks like his leg is the worst of it. I think the motor crushed several bones. We'll know more when Doctor Cannish looks at him. He is conscious and alert, so that is a good sign," said Luke.

Lord Thetford and I hurried over to Miro, laid out on a makeshift cot. He peered up at our approach and a look of relief washed over his face.

"Brother, I am okay. My leg hurts something terrible, but I think I'll live. I just don't know what happened. The accelerant was tested, Gregory checked it over again this morning. I just don't understand," Miro said.

I looked at Luke, and he was talking to an officer excitedly. I walked over to him.

"Luke, we need someone to find Gregory Callen. He is involved, and not just in this accident," I said.

"What do you mean, Belle? What have you discovered?"

"Gregory Callen is Lady Thetford's servant, even from before her marriage. Lady Thetford denied being at the hospital to visit Whitmore, even though you and I both saw her. She used to be Whitmore's school chum before he gave her a prediction she didn't like. Callen's buckles chime like fairy bells! Don't you see?"

"Calm yourself. Even if Callen was chasing Whitmore around, how does that prove he killed those women?"

I looked up and then down and then to my side. My eyes locked on Lord Thetford comforting his brother.

"Oh my gosh! It's both of them!"

"Both of whom, Belle?"

Just then, another officer came up.

"Constable Weston, we have good news. One-eyed Whitmore is awake! He wants to talk to you, and only you," he said.

Luke looked at me and then at Miro being packed up into the back of the wagon.

"Go, it's fine. I think he will only confirm what I predict, but have your officers look for Lady Thetford and Gregory Callen. I think I know what is going on. We can't let them get away," I said.

"Will you be okay?"

At his question, Purgatorio chuffs and sticks out his feathery chest.

"You keep her safe, beastie, or you'll have to answer to me."

He ran toward the wagon as they closed the back doors and prepared to leave. He jumped in and raced off to the hospital.

Nathan came running out of the tunnel.

"Where have you been? Are you okay? Why are you covered in grime?"

"Ah missus, don't be upset. I'm okay, just got caught unawares is all. I was hiding in the race track motor hall, where Mr. Nassar's gear is kept as you said, and I heard someone coming in. I went to hide in the closet, then whoever came in wheeled a tool chest that was next to me in front of the door. I heard some concrete scraping and unlatching metal from under where the tool chest had been, then they ran away. I could tell they were running because of the jingling metal like their boots weren't buckled tight," he said. "I was able to get out when one of the motor hands came looking for something to put out the rest of the fire."

I brought Nathan to me in a big hug. A fierce need to protect him overwhelmed me. I was so glad the intruder hadn't checked the closet, or I might not be hugging Nate now.

"I am glad you are safe. I need you to do one more thing for me. Find my cousin. He had to go to the loo and never returned, and I fear he is in danger," I said.

Lord Thetford stepped towards us.

"Actually Annabelle, I saw him right before the crash. I apologize for only telling you now, but he said he didn't want to ruin the race for you. He said he was feeling quite ill, and he needed to go home. He wanted me to assure you he didn't drive himself, and that he hired a motor," he finished.

"We must go there at once." I whistled for Purgatorio, and he landed on my shoulder. "Nate, let's go hail a cab and get home, post haste," I said.

"Oh, nonsense. I can drive you home. There have been enough close calls today, I don't want to see another *friend* hurt," he said.

I nodded. I felt safe enough with both Nathan and Purgy there to negate any advances from Lord Thetford. I was so wrapped up in unraveling the case, that I did not see the glee in his eyes.

We pooled into Lord Thetford's luxurious motor, and he adjusted the seat for his tall frame.

"Callen usually drives us about." He said as a way of explaining.

He started the motor when I didn't reply. Purgatorio sat between us in the front, and Nate sat in the back. We headed out of the parking stall and down toward the shopping district. All the vendors were still going about their day as nothing had happened. I guess for them, nothing had. Lord Thetford pulled up to the curb outside Claymore's, and I turned to him in question.

"If your cousin is ill, should we not bring him some soup? This place has the best, and always fixes me when I'm ailing," he said.

"Young sir, here's some coin, go inside quickly and get some soup for poor Mr. Nethersby. And don't dawdle, please, I can tell Miss Sweeting is anxious to see her cousin."

Nate took the money and scurried out of the back seat. He entered the store, and before the door closed behind him, Lord Thetford was pulling away from the curb.

"What are you doing?"

"Whatever I want to, Annabelle. Whatever I want."

34

Chapter 34- Cause and Effect

The one who allows their appetite to outweigh their reason has surely damned us all.

Lord Thetford shifted the motor to a higher gear and reached for my leg. Purgatorio hissed and lashed out at Lord Thetford. Several deep red cuts emerged on his hand. Lord Thetford swerved the vehicle sharply, then righted it.

"You bloody piece of rubbish! I'll fix you right!"

Purgatorio coiled his tail back, ready to strike, and then Lord Thetford said it.

"Catacomb!"

Purgatorio turned his head to me, and his eyes faded to black as he shut down instantly. I reached out to hit his nose button, but Lord Thetford slammed the manticore backward between the seats, making it so I couldn't reach Purgy. He turned the motor onto a road that led farther from town. Blood dripped from his hand as he placed it firmly on my knee.

"You think I didn't know about the shutdown code? Miro doesn't make a move without me seeing it. He thinks he's his own creator.

He is what I say he is. Now, isn't this better, Annabelle? We can get to know each other more. We'll just head to a quieter place. All this excitement clearly has you out of sorts."

"Lord Thetford, take me back to town this instant! I don't know what you think you're doing, but it will not end well," I said.

"You have it all wrong. It will end just how I want it to."

"Don't you understand? You are to blame!" I shouted at him.

"What are you talking about, Miss Sweeting? What are you blaming me for, now?" He smirked.

"You had an affair with Gwen Vannery, didn't you?"

"So, what if I did? I didn't do anything to that girl that she wasn't asking for. Like you've been asking for all week."

My stomach roiled at his declaration, but I couldn't let my fear derail me.

"You also had an affair with Katherine Hayes, didn't you?"

"You seem to know a lot about my activities, Annabelle. Are you looking forward to being added to the list, then?"

"She died pregnant, you know? Was the child yours?"

This gave him pause.

"What do you mean, she was with child? How far along?"

"Five months, give or take."

A look of shock and then sadness overtook his features.

"I was told I couldn't have children. Katherine must have cheated."

"Doubtful, she was bragging about her high society gent to her bandmates. Probably thought you would bring her up in the world with your heir in her belly. Who told you that you couldn't have children?"

"My wife's doctor. We've been trying for years. They said it was my fault, something with my genes," he replied.

"You are so blind. Don't you get it? Your wife is having these women killed, clearing the path of any competition," I screamed. "Your delicate Talia is a viper of the first water."

His hand squeezed tighter on my leg. I winced as his fingers dug into my flesh through my clothes.

I forced his hand off my knee, and he cocked it back to strike me. I let the dagger spring from my bracer and directed it toward his throat. He put his hand back on the wheel and gunned it trying to throw me off-kilter. I smiled back at him as my firm grasp didn't waiver. I held it at his neck and demanded he pull over.

He started to slow down, and I felt relief at my impending escape. But when we moved through an intersection to park on the road, a motor slammed into our side.

"What the bloody hell?"

Lord Thetford sped up to get away from the pursuer. It raced alongside us for several more seconds before slamming into us again. This time, causing Lord Thetford to lose control and veer into the ditch.

His body flailed towards mine at impact, and my dagger embedded into his side. I hit my head on the door frame and started seeing stars. The other vehicle pulled to a stop and backed up.

I knew I had to move quickly. Lord Thetford was distracted, staring down at his wound. I stretched myself towards the back of the motor, reaching for Purgy's nose. I struggled to see straight as my own blood dripped down my face. I reached out my hand and pressed his nose.

One, two, three. My passenger door opened. Purgatorio's eyes opened.

"Find Luke!"

I shouted as I was dragged out of the motor by my feet. I landed on my backside, dumped unceremoniously on the ground. Purgatorio tore out of the open door and up into the sky.

Gregory Callen stood over me with a wicked smile. Lord Thetford peered out the open passenger door at us.

"Callen, what in God's name are you doing?"

"Lord Thetford, sir, you've been quite indiscreet. We thought the others would be warning enough, but you don't seem to learn. Talia is none too pleased."

He looked from him to me.

"Yes, a fine little Fate, indeed. You like Botticelli, Miss Sweeting? He's my favorite. Looks like you're going to make another great reproduction. Well, after you've had a chat with the lady, of course," he snickered.

My head swam as he came closer. I lashed out, but he slammed me in the head, causing me to fade to darkness. The last thing I saw as I fell to the ground was Purgatorio in flight. I never needed a mythical creature more on my side than at that moment.

35

Chapter 35- The Woman Behind the Wrath

A man's lust will always lead to a woman's wrath when it strays. That there is still surprise at this truth is remarkable.

I was walking, or gliding, I'm not sure which, through a door. Katherine Hayes played a sad tune on her violin but smiled when she saw me enter. She put the instrument down and ran to embrace me. We twirled like children do when they want to get dizzy. No words were spoken. She gently caressed my face with her hand, then led me out of the room. On a stairway outside sat Gwen Vannery. She was sewing an old, tattered garment. She looked up and smiled softly. I made to sit beside her, and she shook her head no. Gwen pointed toward a closed door at the far end of the hall, light streaming from the crack below. I hesitated, not wanting to leave her. She shook her head more firmly, directing me to the doorway. She finally spoke in a hallowed echo. Her pale finger was cast towards me.

"You need to finish this."

I nodded and turned towards the door. I took one more look at Katherine in the doorway and Gwen on the stairs. I squared my shoulders and walked down the hallway alone. The light behind the door became brighter the closer I got. I reached for the doorknob with a shaky hand. The door opened, and the light flooded my senses.

I blinked my eyes several times before the pain registered. My head ached fiercely, and my wrists felt tight and awkward behind me. I was bound. Shaking my hands, they jingled—shackles. The next thing I noticed was the smell. Pungent with petrol, I knew I was in a motor hall. If I had to guess, Miro's.

I finally was able to peel my eyes open. Harsh gaslights were surrounding me in a triangle. A doorway to the outside sat slightly ajar, and I could just make out two voices. The door flung open violently. Talia Thetford walked in, saw that I was awake, and stood before me. She stared at me for a few moments and then slapped me hard across the face with her left hand. I cried out at the shock more than the pain. I guess I hadn't noticed she was left-handed. She dined with her right hand and served tea with it too. Maybe she did that for society, or she could use them both. My head swam in murky waters, trying to think straight.

"You deserve so much more, you whore! Did you think you could just waltz in and take my husband? That your cute little country manners were going to have you riding off into the sunset? He's mine! And to make sure everyone knows it, you'll be our pièce de résistance," she smiled cruelly.

"I don't want your husband. I never did. I don't understand how you could perceive such a thing. Honestly, Talia, I am not a threat to you."

"First, that little violinist, then that maid, and who knows how many others." She continued on like I hadn't spoken, or she couldn't hear me.

"And now some little upstart from the country, of all places. You think you can lay with him, bear his child, and take my place? You are sorely mistaken."

She struck my face again. This time I felt my teeth rattle. I tasted blood on the side of my mouth. I lulled my head down as if I'd passed out again. She took my shoulders and shook me.

"She's out again, Gregory. Do we have anything to rouse her? I want her to feel the pain as we slice her."

"Patience, milady. Let me see if I have some smelling salts in the motor," he replied.

"Oh, I think there might be some in my bag, I'll come with you to check. She's not going anywhere."

The door shut and locked from the outside. I looked up at the garage, still flooded with light. My head was heavy with vertigo. I turned it side to side, searching for some form of escape. I shook my hands behind me in frustration.

Shackles were a pain to open. Back home, a wicked farmer, named Douglas Grubbs, sometimes used them on the animals of his farm. I hated that old coot. So much so, I snuck to his farm one night. He left the key in the barn, and I released the animals. They ended up several miles away at a kind farmer's house. Small victories.

But after that first release, he started keeping the keys with him. A beautiful mare, Rosie, had me tempting fate once more. I got inventive. I was able to let that horse free, but my father had found out. I was not allowed to go to that farm again.

I did learn something important, though. The best tool to get out of shackles was something small, pointed, and metal. My dagger! The sudden hope turned to defeat as I remembered the last time I saw my weapon was lodged in Lord Thetford's side.

The Thetfords really were quite a pair. Two narcissists had formed a toxic cocktail that leaked out into society. And I think Lady Thetford just confirmed why they've, metaphorically, dropped off the airship. I couldn't focus on the whys right now. I needed to get out of these shackles. I hung my head in frustration, the exhaustion caused my arms to feel numb. Then I saw them. My angled belts still hung across my hips, each pocket containing something of worth. I tried to recall what was in each and if it would help me.

"Bobby pins!"

As if realizing my blunder, I shushed myself and sat silently, straining to hear if anyone heard my outburst. My heart was beating so loudly, it was all I could hear. I waited for several moments before exhaling.

I bucked my hips and used my hands through the slot in the back of the chair. I needed to rotate my belt to the back. I counted the pockets with my hands to reach the right one. I flipped open the pocket and strained my left hand inside. I wrapped my hand around one as the door swung open, the rest of the bobby pins falling to the floor.

"Ah, Lady Talia, looks like our little dancer is awake. No need for the salts after all," Callen called out behind him.

I worked the bobby pin into the keyhole, desperate to release the lock pin and my hands from their bondage. Lady Talia walked in with a knife, smiling. The lock sprung, and I smiled back.

36

Chapter 36- To See the Stars

"I saw the lovely things the heavens hold, and we came out to see once more the stars." - Dante Alighieri

Lady Thetford stopped at my expression.

"Why are you smiling? Don't you know you're about to die?"

"Barren, that's what you are," I replied.

I wanted to force her off-kilter.

"What did you just say?" Her eyes flashed lightning. Callen put a hand on her shoulder.

"You can't have children, that is what this is about. You had your doctor blame Oliver, but it's you," I replied.

"You don't call him that!"

"What, Oliver?" I drug the name out slowly.

"Callen, get the motor ready, this is going to take less time than anticipated," she said.

"But Talia, you know I like to watch."

She turned to him and sliced his arm. "Go now! Little Miss Annabelle and I need our girl time. You can have your fun posing her later," she said.

174

He backed away with his hands up in surrender. When he opened the door, I could see that it was dark out now. I wondered how long I'd been there.

He closed the door behind him. The air filled with an oppressive unease.

"I am Lady Talia Everett Nassar, Countess of Thetford, and you are nothing. How dare you speak to me as if we are equals. You and that ridiculous cousin of yours. Well, we won't be bothered with him any longer, I daresay. I do hope he enjoyed that refreshing poison I supplied him earlier. Nothing like lavender to hide the scent. Now, for you, Miss Sweeting. How dare you say my husband's Christian name. I look forward to splitting your pretty little neck," she said.

Rage and fear warred for dominance as I faced off with this cruel woman. Was Jaime okay? Was she lying, or had she killed my best friend in all the world? Rage won out. I narrowed my eyes at her.

"Oliver and I are quite well acquainted. He said so himself. He was even taking me to his little place outside of town when Callen so rudely interrupted," I goaded her.

She advanced on me. I took the shackles in my left hand and swung out at her, They hit her in the jaw, and she staggered back with a yelp.

"Your husband disgusts me, as do you, Talia! If you don't put the knife down right now, I'll leave you the same way I left him, bleeding!"

"What are you talking about?"

"What, didn't your Gregory tell you? He hit us so hard when we veered off the road, the dagger I was using to fend off your husband's advances plunged into his side. Gregory just left him there bleeding," I said.

The venom in my words spilled out with all the emotions I had bottled up. The outrage of being accosted, the fear and anger of being accused and threatened. The fear of Jaime lying somewhere, dying of poison with no one to help him. The injustice of people's wicked lives, pouring into mine with no say on my part.

"I'll deal with him later, it's you that needs to pay now," Talia said.

I staggered back as my head became fuzzy again. She used this moment to launch at me with her knife. I moved backward, bumping into the chair I had been sitting in. I fell into the seat, barely missing her strike at me. I kicked out at her and connected with her abdomen. A whoosh left her mouth as the air smashed out of her. She reeled back, trying to catch her breath.

I got back up. I swung the shackles around me, not aiming. One wild arc made contact with the knife, and it went flying. We both looked after it as it skittered across the floor. She charged at me with her hands and wrestled the shackles from me. Throwing them to join the knife, she faced me once again.

"Looks like I'll just have to strangle the life out of you," she declared.

"You can stop this, Talia. You can see reason. I don't want to hurt you. I have not done anything with Lord Thetford, nor do I plan to," I said wearily.

"Empty words, from a liar. Your actions play out differently. Always laughing with him and dancing with him so closely. I see the secret smiles as he compliments your frocks. I see it all, Miss Sweeting."

At that moment, I knew she had lost all rational thought. She only saw what she wanted to see, and Talia wanted to hurt me, to kill me. So enveloped in her delusion that no amount of speaking would heal her wounded mind or heart.

I touched the wound on my head and pushed the stray hairs back out of my face. Grazing the bloody strands, I smoothed them back to my bun. My eyes grew wide as I felt familiar cold metal. She must have seen something in my features that made her extend both her hands out, aiming for my neck. I grasped the silver hairpin Nathan had made for me. The amethyst gem shone like a comet in the bright gaslights. Her hands reached my neck as I plunged the metal into hers.

Her grasp loosened, and shock took hold of her face. She stumbled backward, clawing at the pin at her throat. She forced it out. Her eyes met mine and went wide. Blood spurted from her wound in irrational amounts, and I screamed at the gory sight. Callen rushed into the room and dropped to his knees in time to catch her descending body. He shoved his finger in the wound, and the bleeding stopped. Callen looked at me with hatred. I knew he couldn't move if he wanted her to live, so I ran for the open door.

I swayed through the door and out into the night. I went as far as I could before dizziness overcame me. I had made it across the parking stalls and out to the edge of the street. I fell to my knees and looked up into the sky. The stars shone brightly, even with the gaslights on the street. After all the blood, some still staining my clothes, it was a beautiful sight to see. I breathed the fresh air deep into my lungs. Something shiny shot across the sky above me. A red light moved towards me, and a screech shattered the night. I fell to my side and lay there. Before I closed my eyes, a pair of blinding orange orbs grew bigger before me. A motor was coming, and I blinked at its approaching lights as I drifted off to oblivion.

37

Chapter 37- Where There's a Will

Some lessons are hard-fought, some never learned, and some never wanted.

I was floating, no, moving. I was jostled in the back of a motor as my head was held in someone's lap. Soothing words seeped into my brain, and gentle caresses smoothed my hair back from my face. I opened my left eye, then slowly my right. There, above me, was Luke.

"She's awake!"

"Thank God! Hang in there, cousin. We are almost to the hospital." Jaime said from the front seat. His tone was strained.

I felt relief wash over me at his voice. I tried to speak, but nothing came out.

"Ah missus, I'm so sorry!"

"None of that, young Starling. You could not have known what Lord Thetford was about. Thank God for Purgatorio, though," said Jaime.

I tried to sit up, but Luke shushed me and held me still.

"No, no darling. You need to rest. We don't want to stress your body any further. We'll be there soon," Luke said.

One hand stayed on my head and the other held my hand. He brought it up to his face and leaned into it. His features revealed both his fear and relief.

From my vantage point, I could see up into the sky. Purgatorio flew alongside the motor, roaring with urgency. I took my hand from Luke and placed it on the cool window glass, reaching out to my savior. In one way, the Thetfords tried to destroy me, in another, they saved me. For all of Lord Thetford's condescension to Miro, and blaming him for the disgrace of their name. It was Oliver, in the end, that led to their destruction. Would the sins of the brother taint Miro? Sadness overwhelmed me as I already knew that answer. I faded into darkness again.

The next time I awoke I was in a hospital bed. Doctor Cannish was tapping sensors and twisting dials on some shiny instrument. My eyelids fluttered several times before I could combat the weight of them. My mouth was parched, and my jaw and head still ached.

"Ah, Miss Sweeting. Looks like you just couldn't stay away. Best keep these visits to a minimum, or the tongues will start wagging," he joked.

I heard a noise from my right and turned my head to find Luke leaning towards me in a chair. He had his head on one hand, eyes closed, and his other hand holding mine.

"He refused to leave. Said you needed police protection, and all that. Seems he is doing a poor job right now, though," Dr. Cannish said.

"Can I have some water, please?" My voice, hoarse from misuse, croaked out the words.

"Ah, of course. Yes, my dear. Let me fetch that for you."

"What, what? I'm awake. Belle?"

"It's okay, Luke. I'm okay. I feel like an airship crashed into me, but I think I will recover," I said.

"I should never have gone to Whitmore. I should have stayed with you. He didn't tell me anything you didn't warn me about before I left," he said. "He admitted it was Gregory Callen that attacked him. Apparently, Lady Thetford was convinced he knew it was her because of the prediction he gave her years ago.

No matter how she tried, that no legacy would be hers. Any man she married would end their line with her."

I nodded.

"Yes, I figured that out too. Lord Thetford almost did continue his line with Katherine, though. It seems Whitmore's prediction had more than one meaning. What happened to them?"

"The Thetfords? Well, when we found you on the road, it didn't take us long to find Lady Thetford and Callen in Miro's garage. He saved her life. His devotion to her is beyond obsessive. They were taken in the hospital wagon, his finger stuck in her neck the whole way. A surgeon was able to close up the wound, but just barely. She woke up yesterday shackled to her hospital bed. Lord Thetford survived too," he said with a bit of disappointment.

"Purgatorio found Nathan first at Bread Street. Your cousin Jaime, still quite ill, drove out anyway with Purgy guiding them. They found Lord Thetford with your dagger in his gut and knew you were in trouble. He told them that Callen took you. They wanted to leave him for what he tried to do to you, but Jaime decided his punishment should be drawn out in a cell instead. They took him to the hospital, as they were coming to find me, anyway. Poor Jaime started retching as soon as he got here. The nurse discovered poison in his system that caused it. Luckily, it was not deadly but needed to run its course. Since he made it to the hospital they were able to ease the effects," Luke said.

"The drink."

"Drink?"

"Yes, Lady Thetford gave Jaime a drink at the races. She poisoned him. She needed him out of the way to get to me," I replied. "So Lord Thetford survived as well?"

"Yes, he's in the secure ward with his wife. The nurse has been quite liberal with the sedation as he won't stop his belly-aching. Callen is currently detained in Scotland Yard and awaiting trial. If Lady Thetford does recover, she and Callen will face the gallows. Lord Thetford will be stripped of his title. He probably won't do time, as men of his lineage seem to skate the line of justice. His fortune and assets will go to his brother. A small consolation with the ruination of the family name," Luke said.

"Oh my, how is Miro? How's his leg?"

"His leg is shattered, as is his future, by Constable Weston's account," Miro said from the doorway. He wobbled in on crutches and smiled down at me. His green eyes did not hold the same luster as when we first met. A mix of sadness and regret radiated from them.

"Annabelle, I am so sorry. I had no idea my brother had designs on you. I knew he dabbled with his help sometimes, as some men often do. I had not known the depravity had reached such levels. I don't know what else to say. I am truly sorry," he said.

"Miro, it is not your fault. The blame lies in full with your brother, his wife, and her servant. Do not take ownership of such a wicked mix of sin," I replied.

I reached out my hand, and he held it. He brushed his thumb over my knuckles and looked at me with appreciation.

"Thank you, Miss Sweeting. Your words mean a lot. I think it's clear that Purgatorio is yours, as well. Let me offer him as a gift, and I hope in some way, it will help."

He paused for a moment. "I can see that your heart has veered in direction." He looked between Luke and me. "I can only hope in the future I can be worthy enough to find someone that compares to you," he finished.

He left the room before another thing could be said. I looked at Luke, and he looked at me with soft eyes. He leaned over the bed and kissed my lips. It was a gentle kiss, filled with emotion, and I pulled his collar closer to kiss him back. I kissed him fiercely, not only to relay my affection, but the fact that I wouldn't break. His breath labored when I released him, his deep brown eyes shining.

"Ewww! Ah missus, is this bloke accosting you? Do you need me to pummel him?"

"Ah Starling, can't you see young love blossoming before your eyes? 'Bout time too, I'd say," Jaime said.

Nate, with Purgatorio perched on his shoulder, walked into the room with my cousin. They each held flowers. I wanted to cry, I was so happy.

"Oh cousin, I am glad you are okay. That dreadful woman poisoned you, and told me you were dead. And Nate, I am so glad you followed Purgy to me." Tears started to form in my eyes.

A chuff from Purgatorio drew my attention.

"Of course, you too, Purgy! My knight and shining manticore, leading me out of the circles of hell, like Virgil himself!"

"Oh Belle, none of that. We are all safer now, thanks to you. Your bravery with Lord Thetford and quick thinking to send Purgatorio. Your undeniable strength getting away from Talia and her henchman. If I wasn't proud enough before, I am simply overflowing now," Jaime gushed.

"That's right, missus! You're not a Glimmer, nor a Brass. You're the shiniest gem in the crown jewels. You're a Gemmer!"

I smiled at them all. My family—my saviors. My heart swelled with so many emotions. My cousin was right. I had overcome the insurmountable and fought through my own circles of hell. I knew that I could face anything this world presented to me, as long as my makeshift family was there to support me. I knew the stars would shine a little brighter tonight.

38

Chapter 38- Resolution

The past is for victims, the present for survivors, and the future for thrivers.

One fortnight later

***

"Here you go, cousin. Charles had quite the surplus of scraps for you while you were laid up," Jaime said.

He set down my rucksack, filled to the brim with metal bits. My heart fluttered at the pieces I could make with them.

"I also threw in some fancy gears from the shop. It turns out Nate was right about that race. I won a nice little sum as the cars had finished the race before Miro's motor exploded."

"And how was Mr. Kaplan? Happy to see you, I bet," I said.

I wasn't going to let him pass over that bit so quickly.

"Cousin, you need to work on your slyness, it is atrocious. He was quite amiable and will be coming over for our dinner party. I suspect we can also invite Constable Weston to attend, but you probably already invited him, I am sure," he replied.

"Cousin, It is no secret we are courting. You need not tease me for things that are now out in the open. Yes, he is invited, as are the new

Lord Thetford, Whitmore, Lord and Lady Bergenhalt, Lady Whipley and the Cosswald daughters."

"Just the daughters?"

"You know Lord Cosswald can't stand Whitmore, and besides, I don't think I can take that bell of his," I quipped.

Jaime laughed at that. He came behind me and stroked my hair.

"I know you are to become rich and famous with your commissions for Lady Bergenhalt, but I hope you don't leave too soon. I would miss you terribly."

"Who knows? You might need room for a smithy roommate." I smiled at the pouty look he gave me.

"Oh cousin, it will be quite a long time before I leave, and I am not rushing into anything now. Perhaps the older gentleman next door will move to the country and we can be neighbors," I said.

"What an excellent notion, indeed."

Stewart walked into the room behind Jaime.

"A Mr. Weston to see you, miss. He's in the parlor. Shall I have the staff bring tea?"

"Yes, please Stewart. Thank you," I replied.

"Well cousin, I let myself off to the library. I think you've earned a little intrigue. Don't tell your parents how bad a guardian I am, or they'll have you carted back to the country immediately," Jaime said.

I swatted his arm.

"Intrigue, indeed. I only write about the good things, you know that."

We left the room together and parted ways in the hall. I entered the parlor and took in Luke's strong form leaning by the fireplace. He stared into the flames searching for an answer among the embers.

"Good afternoon, Luke. How are you? Or should I say, Inspector Weston?"

He turned to me and smiled, his eyes lighting up as I walked closer. He bridged the gap and brought me in for a hug. He pulled his head back, and I leaned up to look at him. Luke kissed me tenderly. When the kiss was broken, I looked into his eyes and saw worry.

"What's wrong, Luke?"

"Chief Inspector Farthing has another case for me."

"So soon?"

"I'm afraid there are no breaks when it comes to crime," he said sadly.

"Well, I'll come with you."

"No, love, not after what you've just been through. I couldn't ask you to, nor would I want to."

"You didn't ask, I offered. I am made of stronger stuff than you think, Luke. Besides, you need me," I said.

"In more ways than one I assure you, but I don't want you wrapped up in more darkness."

I blushed at that but would not be derailed.

"If you are going, then I am too. It's best just to take my help and not vex me. I'm sure Chief Inspector Farthing would agree after the last case," I said coyly.

"You cannot be talked out of it, then?"

"No."

All of a sudden, the side door burst open.

"If the missus is going to catch criminals, we're coming too!"

Nathan and Purgatorio stumbled forward from the door they'd been eavesdropping at. Purgatorio roared his agreement and took flight towards the vaulted ceiling.

"We're a team, you see? Sweeting and Starling. Ain't we, missus?"

"That we are, Nathan, that we are. So Luke, are you ready to crack this next case with a few extra hands, and er, paws?"

"It doesn't look like I have much of a choice, does it? And you know what, that beastie has grown on me. If it wasn't for him, I'm not sure we would have found you in time," he said.

He looked at me with such raw emotion. I took his hand in mine and squeezed. I wanted to reassure him that we were in this together and that I felt the same way. We stood smiling at each other like fools.

Purgatorio swooped down and landed on Luke's shoulder.

"I guess he's grown to like you too," I laughed.

Purgy chuffed in Luke's ear, making him jump. We all started laughing at that.

Yes, there would be darkness—but there would be so much more light.

The End.

Afterword

If you enjoyed reading this, please leave a review on Amazon or Goodreads. I read every review, and they help new readers discover my books.

Thanks,

LK Billips

About the Author

LK Billips lives in Wisconsin with her wonderful husband and daughter. She has a BA in Comprehensive Art and Certificate in Museum Studies. While art has been a staple in her life, the passion for writing could be ignored no longer. She enjoys crafting, going for walks by Lake Michigan, and playing with her fur babies, Gizmo and Mr. Darcy.

You can connect with me on:

- https://lkbillips.com
- https://www.facebook.com/LKBillips
- https://www.instagram.com/lkbillips

Subscribe to my newsletter:

- https://lkbillips.com

Also by LK Billips

The Compass

https://storyoriginapp.com/giveaways/ ae34fe86-9e7e-11ec-b0f6-038473eefef9

This prequel tells the back story of Jaime Nethersby. The carefree, fun-loving cousin of Annabelle Sweeting hasn't always had it easy. His childhood has been wrought with dark memories, and some questionable family gatherings. This short story gives you a glimpse on how their friendship began, how Jaime came to his current vocation, and how their family bond was made stronger than ever. This can be read before or after The Catalyst.